Strange People, Scary People

Horror Fiction for and about Strange and Scary Entities

By Tally Harbour

Strange People, Scary People
By Tally Harbour

Cover Design by Ginny Glass
Harbour Press Logo Design by Brandon Thomas

ISBN-13: 978-0-578-38435-1

Also available in ebook format.
Published by Harbour Press
tallyharbour2@gmail.com

Printed in the United States of America.

Publisher's Note
This is a work of fiction. Names, characters, places, and incidents either are the product of the author's imagination or are used fictitiously, and any resemblance to actual persons, living or dead, business establishments, events, or locales is entirely coincidental.

The publisher does not have any control over and does not assume any responsibility for author or third-party websites or their content.

For the lovely soprano from England, Sarah.

Contents

GLENDY WITH THE IRON TEETH 1

COOTIES 25

PROFESSOR PATCHWHITE'S GARDEN 33

COUSIN PETE'S ARMADILLO FARM 41

REBECCA'S HAND 53

THE TREE 65

PUMPANDUMP VERSUS PITCHINDITCH 75

DORIAN NECROMANCED 91

OUT OF THE PLEIADES 103

ANAVRIN 139

PINE TREES 149

PROCEDURE MONOMANIA 157

THE WOMB AND THE WINDOW 167

SHE OF THE OTHER KINGDOM 179

Acknowledgments

Life is just one grand, exciting carnival. I am, however, stuck in the scary house.

Yes, that is my situation. And so I write horror short stories. You will read fourteen of them in this book. This book, by the way, was written *about* strange and scary people, *for* strange and scary people. And this, my friend, includes you. After all, you bought this thing, did you not? Anyway, this anthology would not have been possible without the encouragement and help of several wonderful people. First of all, I would like to thank my parents, Tal and Laneve, for supporting me during the years I composed this work. And then there are my sisters, Sherry Allen and Donna Thomas—as well as my brother-in-law, Terry Allen—who never stopped encouraging and assisting me in any way they could. I would also like to thank my good friend, Amos Jones, for all of his assistance. I would like to especially thank Diane Helfrich, whose help was absolutely indispensable. Finally, I would like to mention all of the other family members and friends in Meridian, Mississippi and elsewhere who encouraged me to keep writing. Well, I did, indeed, keep writing; and here is the result. So, read on, my friend—and don't let the haints get you!

GLENDY WITH THE IRON TEETH

I remember many a night a long time ago when my two younger brothers and I would fight for the middle position in the huge feather bed the three of us shared. We each wanted somebody on both sides for many good and scary reasons: reasons such as ghosts, goblins and other spooky things that flitted and crept all about the old house we lived in.

Oh, Mother and Daddy would tell us that the noises we heard around us were merely from the old house creaking and settling, but we knew better. We knew that every *crack* we heard was really old Ned Nobble, who lived inside the walls, cracking his knuckles. He cracked his fingers when he was planning some sort of mischief. Then there was old Sam Scratch, who lived up in the chimney. You were safe from him as long as the fire burned strongly, but when it died down, you had better look out, for then he could come down the chimney and get you. Sometimes we could hear him howling up there. Our parents assured us that the noise was only the sound of the wind blowing down through the chimney, but we knew it was really old Sam Scratch up there howling away.

There just were goblins everywhere. You could sometimes hear their little feet scurrying around in the attic, inside the closets, and sometimes even under our bed. Is it any wonder, then, that each one of us wanted to sleep in the middle?

In time I outgrew these mentioned goblins, but there was one that came to me—it was long after I was over Sam Scratch and his friends—that was so terrifying to me that the mere memory of her can still to this day send a shudder through me. Especially do I tremble when, at night, I hear an owl. Her name was Glendy, Glendy Gray; but we came to call her "Glendy with the Iron Teeth."

We heard the legend of Glendy from the person herself; and she seemed to be just the kind of person that would find great delight in the telling of scary stories to young children. She did more than that, however. Much more, as you will see.

She was a middle-aged woman who, ever since her father had died, had lived all by herself deep in the woods in the small, well-built log cabin her father had constructed. Although we gathered from her Northern accent that she was not from our part of the country, that was just about the only thing that anyone in our little rural community of Suqualena, Mississippi knew about her. And Miss Glendy must have desired being secretive, for she kept to herself, associating with us only when necessary.

Because she still carried her father's name, we could at least presume she had never married. Nor did we expect her to ever marry. And this was not only because she seemed to prefer living in solitude, but it was also because a still single woman in her thirties back in those long-ago early century times was already an old maid. And it was commonly believed that when once a female had attained that terrible status, she was doomed to retain that status until she died. It was even more tragic if the woman happened to be attractive; for this suggested that there was something "wrong" about her—some "flaw" that caused her to shun the company of men, or vice versa. Thus we believed there was something wrong with Miss Glendy, for she was quite attractive.

Her tall, slender frame she expressed well in both carriage and clothing—the latter always being a dark gray, Puritan looking attire that covered her from neck to ankles. Her face was pleasantly oval and just a tiny bit full with carved, classic features. Her eyes were large—and so icy blue that we could not help but wonder if they actually felt frigid to her. In contrast to her pure ivory skin was coal black hair, which always flowed unheeded down her back. Never did we see it pinned or restricted in any manner; and this was yet another point against her. Understand that back in those long-ago Southern days, unpinned hair worn in public by a grown woman was next thing to taboo.

We witnessed Miss Glendy only when it became necessary for her to buy provisions from Mr. Chatam's general store. Once or twice a month she would emerge from the woods and enter the store to purchase food, kerosene, cloth or other commodities.

Nobody knew where the money she used came from, although some claimed that the devil himself gave it to her. When she arrived at the store, which was the favorite place for our people to congregate and gossip, all talking died to whispers and then ceased entirely as she silently conducted her shopping. Resolutely, almost defiantly, she walked among us, picking out what articles she needed and placing them in her wicker basket. And if she happened to catch a stare from anyone, she returned such a total, crushing stare in return, that the initial one was obliterated. In complete silence she trod among us, not even her footsteps making sounds. And this was because, even in the winter, her feet were always bare.

With little, if any, words to the clerk, Miss Glendy would purchase what she had come for and leave immediately, all eyes following her as she crossed the dirt road, headed down the path opposite the store and faded from sight into the forest.

Naturally many rumors had grown among us about her. Some said she was crazy; others claimed that she was "the devil's child." Some offered that she was merely a poor, lonely person whom fate had treated unkindly. But whatever the people in Suqualena thought about her, all agreed that she was certainly a very strange person.

Now let me tell of how three of my childhood friends and I once came to actually visit with Miss Glendy—and why, for a long time thereafter, I refused to sleep near a window.

The adventure began one day in a long-ago spring day when part of the local gang—Tommy, Nathan, Kenny, little Johnny and me—was in conversation behind Mr. Chatam's general store. Sitting on old flour barrels, we were discussing, among other things, Miss Glendy.

"I tell y'all she's a witch! I'll lay my life she is!" swore Tommy, who, at eleven years, was senior among us and self-proclaimed leader of our gang. "Anybody can see she is."

"Aw, she's just a ole crazy woman who don't like people," claimed Nathan. "Ain't no such thing as witches anyways."

"Says who!" demanded Tommy.

"Says my daddy," Nathan proudly replied. "That's who!"

"Aw, yore daddy just says that 'cause he's the preacher—and thinks he knows it all," Tommy chided.

Nathan, for lack of a better reply, responded, "Oh, yeah?"

"Yeah!" Tommy affirmed.

"Yeah!" echoed little Johnny. Because Tommy was his hero, little Johnny would take his side against anything; even against what a preacher said.

"Y'all just go up to her ole shack one night," Tommy continued, "and you'll see her boilin' up sump'n wicked and nasty in that big ole black witch pot she's got. I swear yuh will!"

"And just how do you know she's got a witch pot?" I asked him.

"I just do, damn it! I just do, that's how!" Tommy was the first, and so far, the only one of us who had dared to adopt the habit of cussing. "She cuts up snakes and rats and bats and stuff like that and throws it all in her witch pot and pours in swamp water and stirs it all 'round and cooks it. She even caught ole Hezikia and cut him up and throwed *him* in there and cooked 'im!"

Hezikia was an old servant once employed by the "rich" family in Suqualena, the William Summers household. One night he had gone off to the swamp to do some fishing, but did not return. Nor was he ever seen or heard of again. Naturally we kids had romanticized the disappearance, connecting it to Miss Glendy.

"Gollee!" exclaimed Kenny. "That poor ole fella!"

"Aw, that's just hog slop!" Nathan was still skeptical. Miss Glendy didn't git Hezikia. It was a panther or cottonmouth that got 'im, that's all. What do you think about it, Benji?"

"Gosh, Nate, I don't know *what* to think," I replied. "They searched the woods and the swamp real good for 'im, but couldn't never find nothin'. Ole Man Summers even paid 'em to drag the creek for him, but nothin' never showed up. And even if it was a panther or sump'n that got 'im, they'da probably found some bones or sump'n. I just don't know *what* could'a happened to 'im.

"Well, *I* know what happened to 'im," stated Tommy. "Miss Glendy got 'im—'cause she's a witch—and throwed 'im in her big ole black witch pot!"

"And I still say she *ain't* no witch!" Nathan protested. "And she ain't got no witch pot, neither."

"She has *too*!" cried little Johnny. "She has *too* got a witch pot—'cause Tommy goes up there at night and hides and spies on her and watches her stirrin' in her witch pot—'cause he tole me he does! *Ain't* that so, Tommy! *Ain't* you been to spy on her? *Ain't* you seen her witch pot! Tell 'em!"

We looked with incredulity, and disdain, at Tommy, who, with hands now jammed in his pockets, was looking at the ground and shuffling about as if he were suddenly seized with no little discomfort.

"Tell 'em so, Tommy!" Little Johnny was still pleading. "Tell 'em you been to spy on 'er!"

"That's a lie!" accused Nathan. "You ain't never spied on Miss Glendy."

"I—I have, too," Tommy stammered. "I have too been to spy on her."

"Aw, you're lying!" I claimed. "You ain't never in your life been to spy on her. You ain't got no more guts to go up there alone at night and spy on Miss Glendy than none of us."

"He has too got the guts!" Little Johnny seemed almost ready to jump on me for assailing his hero's integrity and courage. "Take 'em with you, Tommy. Just take 'em with you when you go up there to spy on her again, and show 'em you got some guts." Little Johnny was getting his hero into more and more difficulty.

"Uhh...well, uhh... I tell yuh, Johnny...uhh... I kinda decided to quit goin' in them woods no more 'cause...uhh...'cause, yuh see—it's them skeeters. Yeah, them skeeters are gittin' terrible bad now; and I'm skeered that if I get bit too many more times, I'll take terrible bad sick." This was Tommy's pitiful, hardly audible reply to his young worshiper.

We were overjoyed to witness the big bragger finally tangled up in one of his own yarns. He was completely helpless in front of us and his six-year-old devotee. For many moments following his pathetic response, he remained in mute misery, his eyes focused on the dust stirred up by his restless feet.

But then he suddenly looked up at us and blurted, "Hell! I don't want to go and git myself cut up and cooked in no witch pot!"

"Take 'em, Tommy! You just gotta go and show 'em!" Little Johnny was almost in tears. For it is the youngest among us who become the most distressed when flaws and fissures appear in golden idols. "Please, Tommy, *please!* You just gotta go and take 'em and show 'em you ain't skeered."

"Yeah, Tommy," snickered Nathan, "take us to spy on her and show us you ain't skeered." All of us, Nathan included, most certainly considered the prospect of trekking off through the woods with the intention of spying on Miss Glendy just as dreadful as did Tommy; but Nathan, who was not worried about the possibility of any of us actually undertaking such a frightful venture, could not resist the opportunity of help sink big shot Tommy deeper into his quagmire.

Tommy, however, feared losing face just as much as he feared Miss Glendy. As Nathan, Kenny and I taunted him and dared him to take us to her cabin, he suddenly shouted, "Alright, damn it, alright! I'll go! We'll *all* go and spy on her, and I'll prove to y'all she *is* a witch!"

Now it was suddenly the turn of his three deriders to feel trapped and dismayed. Not expecting Tommy to actually take us up on our dare, we found ourselves wishing that we had not made such an issue of this. And Tommy, who noticed how disconcerted we had become, took full advantage of it. Now it was *his* turn to put the pressure on.

"Yeah, we'll go—that is if *y'all* ain't yella."

The four of us were already dangerously entangled in this frightful enterprise even before the term "yella" had been introduced in the discussion, but now that it had been entered, all hope of escape was lost. If any of us decided to back out of this, he would, from that day forward, carry upon himself this terrible label. And to Southern lads, especially young Mississippians, there is no worse degradation.

So it was eventually agreed that the four of us would meet here the following day, Friday, after school. We decided, also, to tell our folks we desired to camp out. This would save them any worry in case we were late arriving home. Our mission: travel to Miss Glendy's cabin and hide and spy on her.

Although he begged us to take him with us, little Johnny was too young to be included. And although he told us how proud he was to have such brave kids as us as his friends, his honest desire to go with us proved him to be the bravest of the lot.

"Daddy, what do you think Miss Glendy is?" I asked at the supper table that night. "*Is* she a witch?"

"Benjamin! What a sinful thing to ask about someone!" my mother chastised. "Miss Glendy is just a poor lonely woman who just never learned how to socialize with people."

"Well, Mother, how come so many people say she's a witch, then?" My two younger brothers, whom the subject also interested greatly, heartily voiced their interest and agreement with me. After they finished, I continued, "And besides, don't witches always like to live alone like she does?"

Here my father chimed in, "That's true, Katherine. Lots of the folks around here claim she's a witch. And even those that say she ain't one are still skeered of her—even ole Joe Hash, who says that ghosts and witches and stuff like that are sump'n only fools believe in.

"Why, I remember one night when me and him was rabbit huntin'. We were walkin' 'long that trail that starts over by the general store and were real deep in the woods. Well, suddenly we hear this singin' coming from way off yonder in the swamp somewhere. It warn't bad singin,' neither. Right pretty it was. But it was also kinda different from most singin' that yuh hear. Kinda spooky like yuh might say. Well, when we rec'lected that it just might be *her*, Miss Glendy that is, singin' that song—and I think it was 'Barbara Allen'—ole Joe suddenly says that his leg—you know, the one with the Yankee musket ball still in it—is startin' to pain him, and that if he don't get home real soon and soak it in vinegar, it'll pain 'im for months on end. Well, I went along back with him to keep him company. And I can't say that I was that reluctant to go, neither, 'cause that singin' sent a shiver down my spine, too. We headed on home, but at the pace ole Joe took out through them woods gittin' out of there, his leg seemed alright enough to me!"

"Now, Ben, why do you encourage the boy," asked my mother. "You know just as well as I that Glendy Gray is not a witch. And those people who say such things—if they would spend as much time in church as they do gossiping in Mr. Chatam's store, they would learn how sinful and shameful it is to go about spreading wicked rumors about someone."

"You listen to your mother, son," advised my father. "I'll warrant that Miss Glendy's harmless enough." But after a pause, he grinned and added, "But just the same, I wouldn't be all that surprised to learn that she just might use her broom for something other than sweepin' floors!"

He laughed long and heartily at his joke, and I noticed that even my mother tried to resist a smile. I, too, would have probably found it funny—funny that is if it had not been my intention to venture to Miss Glendy's cabin the very next night! In fact, that little joke completely ruined any assurance I had hoped to receive from my parents that there was nothing to fear from her.

"Well, where is he?" Tommy asked the following day. "Is he gonna turn yella on us?"

Sitting on our usual flour barrels behind the general store, we had been waiting on Nathan for over an hour.

"Maybe he told his maw about what we were gonna do today, and she wouldn't let 'im come," surmised Kenny as he sucked on a strawberry candy ball.

"Naw, we warn't 'sposed to tell our folks about it, remember?" I reminded him. "Say, gimme one of them jawbreakers, Kenny."

"Well, whatever happened, he's still yella if he don't come,' declared Tommy.

"Well, I don't care what y'all call me," Kenny said as he tossed me a piece of candy, "but it don't mean I'm yella if I say I ain't goin' in them woods if it gets too much later. I'll be dang if I go in them woods lookin' for Miss Glendy after it gets dark!"

"Yeah, me neither," I agreed as I popped the candy in my mouth. "Besides, we didn't say nothin' 'bout goin' in them woods at night, anyways."

"Well, I sure ain't goin' by myself!" cried Tommy. Then he quickly—and with obvious self-irritation—added, "I mean...uhh... I mean it wouldn't do no good for me to go along without y'all, 'cause then I couldn't prove to y'all that she is a witch like I said."

This hollow explanation was only another example of how Tommy, who had claimed he had spied on Miss Glendy alone and at night, was still caught up in the ridiculous fabrication he had spun to little Johnny. It was the big lie that had entangled us all in this dreadful venture.

But we were now beginning to see some hope of canceling this fearful enterprise and, at the same time, escaping with some measure of honor. Having already proclaimed to each other that we would not venture into the forest if it became too close to night, we conferred and concluded that if Nathan did not appear by six-thirty, we would cancel our trip on account of the lateness of the day, leaving him with the blame. He would be the "yella" one—not us. And as for simply postponing the trip for another time, we decided on the resolution that we were either going today or never. According to Tommy's pocket watch, it was ten minutes after six. So we continued waiting, praying for the speedy arrival of six-thirty without Nathan.

But five minutes before our time of deliverance, our hopes were destroyed when we beheld our planned scapegoat suddenly round the corner of the store.

"Sorry I'm late, y'all, but when I got home from school, my maw made me hang around the house and visit with my aunt, who came to our house today. Then I had to do a bunch of chores."

When no one offered comment, he then asked with anything but enthusiasm if we were still going through with the plan.

"I reckon so," Tommy sighed, looking despairingly at Kenny and me.

"Well, if we're goin', then let's go," Kenny said. Then he spit out a licorice jawbreaker and added, "Let's go 'fore it gits too close to dark. But it was already "too close to dark," for as we departed, the setting sun was already not far from singeing the horizon.

* * *

It was about thirty minutes later, while we were walking down the path through the woods that it occurred to me that none of us had the faintest idea of just how far we had to go to reach Miss Glendy's house. As the other two and I had no confidence in our leader, Tommy, no one cared to ask him. Under different circumstances we would have tested and derided him, but this undertaking was too serious for that. We simply continued to follow him down the trail, no one saying a word.

Eventually the pines and sweet gums bordering the path started giving way to poplar, oak, hickory and sycamore trees. This signaled that the ground was becoming more moist and fertile. Apparently we were near the creek. Suddenly, in perfect unison, the spring locusts began their loud buzzing. It fairly startled us, so unexpected was it; then we recalled, with no little anxiety, that the locusts always begin to sing when the sun starts to set. And, as everyone knows, after the sun sets there is dusk, then darkness.

A few minutes after the locusts began sounding, we reached a foot log spanning a backwater from the creek. While crossing it, we disturbed a huge bullfrog that leaped from his repose on the knee of a cypress tree into the stagnant, filmy water with a great *plop.* I looked way up towards the top of the giant tree and saw no sunlight reflected. The night was certainly coming. This was reason enough to turn back; and all four of us were certainly aware of it. But even at this stage, the dread of the terrible word "yella" hung over all, and thus prevented anyone from proposing a retreat. While any of us, I am sure, would have wholeheartedly seconded the motion, none would bring himself to forward it. So we could do nothing but continue onward.

As we trudged on deeper into the wilderness—now more swamp than forest—the sounds of the denizens of the night began. Joining the locusts in song were myriads of crickets and tree frogs—their chorus augmented by the crisp buzzing of the cicadas and the katydids and the deep bass croaking of the bullfrogs. Several jays flew over us sounding their shrill calls, and a mocking bird whistled loudly close by. Not too far away we heard the harsh yowling of a bobcat—accompanied by the unmistakable screech of a hawk. And, as hundreds of lightning bugs began flickering soft green light everywhere, we heard, from way off in the distance, the sad cooing of a mourning dove. Then, *ha-ha-haoooah…ha-ha-haoooah.* Somewhere, in some tree very close to us, a hoot owl called out.

As one might imagine, the owl had certainly played its part in raising goose bumps on us, but there was yet another sound, a more subtle sound we now heard, that unnerved us even more. I speak of the song of the whippoorwill.

The song of the whippoorwill is at once recognizable—it forms the name of the bird itself—but one seldom sees this animal. Floating on the twilight breeze, its song seems to portray a sad longing, a forlorn desire, perhaps, for something wonderful lost long ago. It is indeed a melancholy sort of sound, and if one listens to it for too long a while, the person may become affected in a like manner. He or she may even become a bit frightened; for the whippoorwill is the most mysterious of all birds, and the many legends that have grown up around all concern ghostly or morbid aspects. Some say that these birds are the reincarnations of people that died of broken hearts. Others claim that the bird is really hinting the words "widow's near." It is a warning that a certain scary old hag that grows older and older but can never die is creeping about—or watching you. Legend has it that she sucked out the eyes of her husband just to see how they tasted and then turned him into a toad with black magic and ate him. They say that she always comes out at dusk and that the whippoorwills follow her around as she creeps through the forest—maybe a forest near *you*—searching for her favorite treat: the eyes of anyone unfortunate to fall into her clutches. So, if you're ever in the woods after the sun goes down and happen to hear a whippoorwill close enough for you to distinctly make out the words of warning, "widow's near," you had better start moving quickly on. And if you ever actually *see* a whippoorwill, you had best start running as fast as you can—and not look behind you.

The gray mantle of twilight had now covered everything. Tommy, still leading, was walking slower and slower, obviously reluctant to continue on, while Kenny, in the most fearful position of the rear, kept crowding my back. Moving just a little bit faster than turtles, it was not long before we were all bunched up together, each of us glancing fearfully around at the darkening shadows.

Then Tommy finally stopped completely and broke the long-held silence with a low, nervous voice. "Listen, y'all, I reckon by now y'all know I ain't never been to spy on Miss Glendy. I don't even know how much further it is to wherever she lives, but I tell yuh, I ain't goin' no further. I ain't yella, neither, but I say we get out of here right now."

"Why, you little men are almost there," came a soft, feminine voice from behind us. "I live just around yon curve."

We jerked around, and to our surprise and extreme terror beheld the form of Miss Glendy standing behind us. Yes, it was her, Miss Glendy, herself: who we had intended to spy on. But she had turned the tables. It was she who had apparently been secretly watching us! And just like a witch she seemed to have materialized from nowhere like magic.

Her appearance paralyzed us like deer caught in bright lights. We could do nothing but keep absolutely motionless, our full moon eyes frozen on her figure.

"Why, I do believe you are afraid of me. Why do I frighten you so?"

Following a long silence, Tommy finally found the courage to respond. "C-Cause you're a witch! That's why! You did something awful to pore ole Hezikia and now you want to do something awful to us, too!"

Miss Glendy then smiled and replied, "There, there, my little man. I've never harmed anyone, and I certainly would not think of harming such nice little men as you and your friends. Come now, please, and visit with me. There's nothing to be afraid of, I promise you. I seldom have guests in my home, so please come. I'll give you refreshment. I'll also tell you a nice little story. Please come with me; you'll like my cozy little cabin."

However wondrous it might have seemed, Miss Glendy's warm, amicable words succeeded in calming much of our terror of her. Maybe she was only "a poor, lonely person," as my mother had claimed, after all. Far from portraying the aloof and scary Miss Glendy of the general store, she now seemed as harmless as the next person.

But notwithstanding her success in quelling most of our fears, we were still a bit uncomfortable in her presence, and quite at a loss as to what to do. Silence reigned until I finally thought of something to say. "Well, I don't know. It's gittin' late, and it's a long ways back home."

She looked at me and smiled again. And even in the gathering darkness, I discerned that her teeth were very pretty, and very white.

"Why, my little man, it's not far at all. There is a much shorter route to the village; and I will show it to you if you will first come with me to my home."

Her charm had now melted away every bit of our apprehension, and we wavered on the verge of acquiescing to her. Then she stepped closer and politely, but with a slight tone of command, said, "Come. You will love visiting with me."

And we obeyed; we followed her. And as she led the way, she hummed a ballad. It was the song that my father had mentioned last night at the supper table. It was "Barbara Allen."

"Have you ever had goat's milk?" Miss Glendy asked. "It's very good—so much better for nice little men than milk from cows."

Tommy, Nathan, Kenny and I were sitting around a circular oak table that supported, along with our four tumblers, a kerosene lamp. Our hostess went around to each boy and filled his tumbler with the milk whether he had expressed a desire for it or not.

Her cabin, I reflected, was probably a lot like the one Davy Crocket had lived in. It was a rectangular, one room structure built of huge oak logs and mud plaster with a roof of wood shingles and a floor of rough-hewn boards. Built within one wall was the hearth which, notwithstanding the comfortable spring evening contained a fire. By the wall opposite the fireplace was a featherbed, and above the bed was the sole window in the building. Jutting out from another wall were shelves containing food and other supplies, and the remaining wall was distinguished by the doorway and a huge chest of drawers. Aside from our four wooden chairs and the large rocking chair in which Miss Glendy reposed, these articles were the entire furnishings in the cabin.

Outside the house, we had noticed that Miss Glendy had as companions three brown goats, ten or twelve chickens and a cat that appeared to be so ancient that it would have trouble doing anything but sleeping. There was also a small garden surrounded by a split rail fence, a well, a shed for her garden implements, and an outhouse. We had perceived no "big ole black witch pot."

"Finish your milk, my little men," she said; "and seat yourselves closer to the fire so that I may tell you the nice little story I promised you."

We gathered our chairs next to the hearth as she had directed, our backs to the fire. Then Miss Glendy, who had said that this was to be a "nice" story, extinguished the lamp, thereby reducing all light in the cabin to only the dim and ruddy, wavering illumination provided by the flames. Then she pulled her rocking chair in front of us, seated herself and began:

"I wonder if you've ever heard of Salem, Massachusetts? Over two hundred years ago the people there used to hang unfortunate young women who they accused of practicing witchcraft. Well, there was a certain other hamlet in New England along that time where they would actually burn accused witches. This town was called "Ashwich." If the people there came to suspect a woman of being a witch, they would arrest her, put her on trial and, as I mentioned, if they judged her guilty, consign her to a terrible death by burning her alive.

"The principal witch hunter of this town was one Zebulon Bannington, a reverend and chief magistrate. This man would put forth his utmost to destroy any who were suspected of being a witch, often arresting them on the shallowest of evidence.

"It so happened that Zebulon came to suspect a young lass named Nellie Lullarey, the daughter of one Maggie Lullarey. Crying, pleading and protesting her innocence, Nellie, having been found guilty, was tied to the stake—her cries falling on deaf, indifferent ears. If any did feel compassion for her, they dared not show it for fear of arousing suspicion among themselves.

"When all was in readiness, Zebulon, wielding a torch in one hand and a Bible in the other, mounted the platform on which Nellie was to be executed. After reading aloud certain scriptures from the holy book to save young Nellie's soul, he stepped back and cast the torch on the brush and wood piled around the condemned. Other torches were quickly added, and a great conflagration soon enveloped the victim.

"'Burn, witch...burn, witch...burn, witch,' chanted the crowd; and poor innocent Nellie screamed in her agony.

"Suddenly there burst from among the spectators Nellie's wailing and disheveled mother, Maggie. And Maggie really *was* a witch. So dreadful and forbidding was her contorted, bloodless face that the people shrank back from her in fear. Then, after mounting the platform, Maggie started wailing out ominous words..."

Here Miss Glendy stood up and, glaring down at us, showed a twisted, frightful expression. And when we beheld it, we did not need to imagine what Maggie must have looked like in her travail. Then Miss Glendy, raising her voice, continued the story...

"'Oh blackest day, oh darkest day, would that thy sun had never risen to have made thee manifest! Would that I had never been conceived! For how is this black time to be endured! Even now I feel my heart bursting!

"'But hear me now, ye people who have seen fit to take my child and deliver her to the flames: this crime shall in no wise remain forever without redress. Retribution shall not forever tarry from thy doorsteps. For there shall come a time when the children here will be taken from their mothers just as my child was taken from me. Nay, not *your* children, nor even *their* children; for this crime must first become only a small incident in the annals of this accursed place. But I speak of the offspring of a generation far in the future. It shall be *their* parents who will have ample cause to regret this vile, vicious deed. They shall come to hate ye, their forbears, with virulence; for truly it is virulence that they shall inherit from ye. I say to them, beware. Beware of the seed of Bannington; for from this man, this person who dared to condemn my Nellie and, yea, cast the first torch, there shall one day spring forth a certain terrible one. A terrible one that on quiet, moonlit nights shall tread softly just without the windows of the sleeping young ones. A terrible one that, from bed or cradle, shall steal away the wee ones and devour them. Neither lock nor bar shall deny it entry; for its strength shall be given it from hell itself. It shall have stealth; it shall have quickness. It shall laugh at the attempts to capture it or destroy it.

Yea, it shall walk among your descendants even under the sun, for it shall be completely safe in their ignorance of its person. Not even its own parents shall realize the true nature of that which they conceived and harbor.

"'The beast shall plague thy descendants until they discover from what linage it was made manifest. Then shall they set upon all of the seed of this Zebulon Bannington and purge that entire clan from their midst. For they must purge them all for the sake of purging one: the unknown creature that preys among their children. And it is only when this is done that your descendants, thinking of their young, shall not fear the night.'

"Having finished her ominous prophecy, Maggie plunged into the flames and embraced her silent, charred daughter. And as if the fire had anticipated her entry, it roared up high and hid the two within from the vision of the onlookers. A long, tortured wail was heard…then there was silence. All believed now that the woman had perished. But suddenly, like a ghostly echo from within the fire the voice of Maggie Lullerey sounded for the final time: *'On quiet, moonlit nights it shall tread softly just without the windows of the sleeping wee ones. On quiet, moonlit nights when the owl disturbs the very soul with the nearness of its scream.'"*

And as Miss Glendy recited Maggie's final words, there was such an eerie quality about her voice that my skin tingled all over. I decided I really did not want to hear any more of this tale. But Miss Glendy continued:

"The voice trailed off near the end; and that was the last of Maggie.

"After the blaze had died, Zebulon ascended the platform and cast holy water on the two blackened remains. But the water sizzled only upon the corpse of Maggie.

"This incident was not easily forgotten by the residents of Ashwich. But as they eventually died out with time, so too did the memory of Maggie and her curse. Years, then decades and finally centuries passed; and during this time the town prospered little and hardly changed. The size of its population was much the same two hundred years later in 1892. It was in the spring of this year when the children began to disappear. The first was a mere infant hardly a year old. And the opened window above its empty cradle was the only evidence of the abduction. The only evidence, that is, until the following morning when a small, neatly arranged pile of tiny, wet human bones was discovered on the ground outside the child's room. Following this, the mother had to be tenderly put away in an asylum, for the shock and grief were too much for her. Before the year was out, three more children were taken, and later returned in the same ghastly manner."

Here Miss Glendy paused for a moment; and, for some reason that I did not want to contemplate, slowly licked her lips. Then she continued.

"Five were taken the following spring despite the efforts to protect them. It was as if whatever was taking the young ones was endowed with magical powers. It did not matter how vigilantly the fathers, armed and desperate to protect their offspring, stood guard over the cradles and beds; for on the nights when the abductor stalked about, the fathers of their victims—as if through witchcraft—fell deeply asleep. And in the mornings, when they awoke to find their children missing, the last thing they could recall about the proceeding nights was the screaming of an owl just outside the windows."

Wondering, at this point, if my three companions were becoming as uneasy as I was, I glanced around at them—and saw opened mouths and wide eyes. It was obvious that they, like me, were quite scared.

"For five years Ashwich was subjected to this terror," she continued. "Suspects were arrested—one even being executed—but the abductions continued, followed always by the grisly mementos.

"Finally, as a last resort, the people decided to heed the advice of a certain old man called Nimrod, a mystic hermit, who for years had been telling them what action to take against the scourge.

"'It is from the old curse of Maggie Lullarey whence this malignancy has its origin,' he advised them. 'Read the record of the incident for yourselves. Read it, and know that to save the children you must, as Maggie proclaimed, rid yourselves of the entire family of Bannington. For just as it is from within that house that the creature has arisen, it is also within that same house that it finds refuge. Aye, they harbor it in innocence; they are as ignorant as you as to its identity. Nevertheless, you must take action against the entire clan; for in so doing you shall eject the beast as well. Take heed. Purge them *all.* For this measure, drastic though it may be, is the only way you will deliver yourselves from this malevolence.'

"For years the majority had been skeptical of this advice, passing it off as mere ravings of a lunatic. Those who did pay it serious thought were filled with apprehension about taking such a severe action. But when the thirty-second child was taken—a mere infant barely two weeks from the womb—the people finally decided to heed old Nimrod's advice. And when once they committed themselves to the deed, the rage and desire for revenge that had been festering for so long erupted. They wanted to do more than simply drive the clan of Bannington from the village. They wanted blood. Ruthlessly they set about the grim task, searching for any unfortunate person with Bannington blood they knew. Some were burned alive in their homes. Others were drug outside and slain in the streets. Even the youngest were shown no mercy; for all were hated like death. In one day the task was completed; and all the members of the previously respected house of Bannington that had not been slaughtered were fleeing for their lives.

"Thereafter the abductions ceased, giving proof that old Nimrod had apparently been correct. The creature, at least in Ashwich, stalked no longer; but what it or who it was, whether it escaped from the wrath of the people of Ashwich, and, if still alive, where it abides today, no one knows."

Here Miss Glendy became silent. The only sound in the cabin was the soft cracking and popping of the fire. Then she fashioned a smile about her lips...very slowly. It could be considered as pleasant, yes, but there was also a hint of something else about it, something mischievous that was a bit unnerving. And that, coupled with the "nice little story" she had related to us, again caused my flesh to creep.

"Gosh!" I exclaimed in a whisper. "That's some story. But it didn't really happen, did it?"

"Oh, yes, my little man. It happened just as surely as you and I are here right now."

She was still smiling at us in that strange way; and it was becoming downright frightening. I decided that I wanted to leave.

"Well…uh, y'all about ready to go?" I nervously asked my three friends.

The others, who I was sure were experiencing the same uneasy emotions as I, immediately signaled that they were ready to leave also. So we then requested Miss Glendy to direct us to the shortcut home she had mentioned.

"But my story is not quite finished," she protested. "You *shall* hear the rest.

"The remaining members of the Bannington family, their homes in ashes and their lives all but shattered, scattered far and wide, all fleeing New England entirely. Some went north into Canada; others went south to such states as Virginia, Kentucky, Tennessee and…" here she paused and again revealed her very white teeth in the same mischievous smile, "…Mississippi. At least one family came here, a man and his daughter. But fearing, even down here in the small community in which they had settled, that the story of their banishment would follow them and cause them trouble, they went under a different name. Even so, they preferred to keep mainly to themselves in their cabin deep in the forest. Years passed, and in 1900 the father died, leaving the daughter all alone. And because she continued to keep to herself, the people of the nearby community began to think there was something strange or unwholesome about her. Some even thought she was a witch, especially the young ones…" And here she paused and again showed those almost unnaturally white teeth in the smile. It was larger than before, but it was no longer pleasant at all. It now looked downright sinister. In growing fear and alarm we looked at each other and then back to her. "…One night four little fools who were trying to prove their bravery, and to discover if she really was a witch, came to spy on her…" She was leaning closer to us, and within her taut, wider than ever grimace, we saw the firelight playing upon teeth which, to our extreme terror we now discovered were absolutely enormous. They looked to be over an inch long. "…After tricking them to come inside her lair, she made them drink goat's milk…." The fire was flickering in her animal looking, hungry looking eyes, her face was contorted in unwholesome ecstasy, and her jaw was slowly sliding and grinding her lower teeth again the upper ones. "…Because goat's milk makes little children's flesh more tender to chew."

Then, HA-HA-HAOOOOAH!

Immediately following her last words—it was as if she had conspired with it—a hoot owl screamed very loudly just outside the window. She followed the owl with an explosion of repulsive, cackling laughter. And meanwhile she was leering at us more hideously than ever, and slowly reaching towards us long, writhing fingers with very long, sharp looking nails.

As the owl screamed, I became aware that we were screaming too. In absolute fright we screamed. In absolute terror we jumped up and away from those wiggling fingers. In absolute panic we stumbled and bounded over each other for the door. We threw it open and fled across the yard and down the path. I was last in the mad race, but pressing the one ahead of me, Nathan, like a crazed quarter horse. And while we ran, we could hear Miss Glendy still laughing behind us. Just before the woods closed the cabin behind me, I cast a terrified glance backward over my shoulder, praying that I would not see her running, or even flying, after us. And then I saw a scene I know I shall never forget. I beheld Miss Glendy out in the yard, her figure silhouetted in the light of a brilliant full moon. With hands on hips and head thrown back she was laughing and laughing, laughing like no human I had ever heard. The mocking, cackling sound chased us, it seemed, forever, slowly growing fainter and fainter until it finally faded away; but it was not until we reached the foot log spanning the slough that we slowed down—and then only because it required caution in crossing it. Feeling a small measure of safety on the other side of the backwater, we paused to rest, all four of us bent over with hands on knees panting, heaving and sobbing. But the nightmare was not over; for it happened that we again heard an owl scream close by, sending us scampering away once more and crying with new terror. And this time we did not stop until we were safe inside Tommy's house, the closest home in which to take refuge.

Even with the aid of the moonlight, it still amazes me how we ever escaped from those woods, running as we were, without getting lost or hurt. But what I find, to this day, as downright unbelievable was the almost indifferent reactions from our parents. The first response came from Tommy's folks. Although we were dripping with sweat and although we were covered with scratches from our wild flight though the woods, Tommy's parents, upon hearing our hysterical report concerning the night's events, decided to accept the story as a wild exaggeration. They told us to calm down, that Miss Glendy had merely played a "harmless joke" upon us, and that no "monsters" were going to get us. And this, as it turned out, was more or less the reaction from all of our parents. They all accepted the incident as some sort of prank. She was just "kidding" us, they claimed, just having a "little fun" with us. They advised us that we were too old to believe in the "bogeyman and stuff like that." But if we were so afraid of Miss Glendy, they added, we should simply, from then on, stay away from her cabin. As if we would ever actually consider going back there again!

Needless to state, we never dared to venture very far down that path again. We stayed far away from her part of the woods; but that was not to be the last time we saw her. For she continued making her infrequent trips to the general store—always with that same cold, indifferent expression on her face. And even if any of her four "little men" happened to be there, she never showed even the slightest bit of recognition. And as for us, if we did not flee her presence entirely, we would retreat behind the backs of any available adults and sneak fearful glances at her.

As time passed, and as Tommy, Nathan, Kenny and I repeatedly related our adventure with her to the other kids, Miss Glendy became even more terrifying. *Of course* she was a witch. That went without saying. But she was also some kind of horrible woman creature from someplace up north called "Ashwich." *Of course* she had got old Hezikia. She had caught him, cut him up, cooked him in her "big ole black witch pot" and eaten him. Yes, we concluded that she did have a pot somewhere. We hadn't discerned it, we decided, simply because she kept it hidden. Yes, she would eat anybody, but preferred kids the most. She was stronger than ten men put together, and had fingernails ten inches long that could punch through leather. But the most terrible thing about her was her mouth. For it contained her teeth. They looked to be over an inch long, powerful and razor sharp. In time we concluded that her teeth were really made of iron, and that to disguise them, she painted them white. Hence her nickname.

Today I still wonder about Miss Glendy. And I wonder if there really is a town called Ashwich up in New England somewhere. I keep thinking that one day I might do some research about it, but I am almost afraid of what I might discover. I try to believe that there was nothing supernatural involved with this person. I try to believe that Miss Glendy was just a warped individual who, perhaps, hated children and liked to tamper with their young minds. But then I remember how naturally and convincingly she had related that story and how easily the words came to her. I remember those grinding, gumless fangs…and I wonder. At any rate, I cannot recall, to this day, the ballad, "Barbara Allen" without shuddering.

"Y'all had better not be sleepin' by the window when the owl starts to scream real close outside," we warned our friends; "'cause that means that Glendy with the iron teeth is lookin' at you through the window—and fixin' to get you!"

Finally, neither I nor anyone else that lived in Suqualena ever found out what eventually became of Miss Glendy. A few years following our adventure with her, it happened that we started to miss her appearances at the general store. After about two months of her absence, some of the men decided to check up on her to see if there was anything amiss. They found her cabin undisturbed but deserted. And I suppose it has remained so ever since, for to my knowledge, she never returned.

COOTIES

Rita Jean Shumate was, without a doubt, the dirtiest kid in the whole of Miss Edward's fifth grade class. She was probably the dirtiest kid in the whole of Webster County Elementary School. She apparently seldom, if ever, took baths. She certainly didn't smell like she ever cleaned herself, and her grubby face, her grimy hands with the filthy fingernails and the dirt beads which always ringed her neck gave evidence of this. She obviously never washed her blond hair, either, for it was always oily and stringy. She always wore the same soiled, tattered blue dress with the faded yellow flowers. And as for shoes, she apparently had only one pair: some green, worn-out sneakers. She only used them when it was cold; when it was warm she went barefoot. And one might only imagine the sight her nasty feet must have presented.

She was a prime example of poor white trash—if there is indeed such a class. And she certainly had cooties. Yes, cooties. Those mysterious crawling little bugs that are always associated with certain people, especially girls, who are considered as being creepy, or loners, or who are just plain gross. And Rita Jean Shumate certainly fit very well into all three of these categories—especially the last.

And all of this was a bit of a shame because, otherwise, she could have been quite a cute little girl.

Her teacher, Miss Edwards, was an old beanpole of a spinster who fervently believed in the old adage, "cleanliness is next to godliness." It was no surprise, then, that she had, time after time, chastised Rita Jean in front of the whole class as to her lack of hygiene. But as yet, she had failed to achieve any results in her student. So one day, she decided to take matters into her own hands.

"Rita Jean Shumate, if you do not start bathing yourself, I just might have to have a little talk with your mother."

And Rita Jean answered, "I'll think about it, Miss Edwards, but taking baths is something we Shumates hardly ever do. Baths just don't seem to go right with us."

At this, the class snickered.

Miss Edwards, irritated by the reply, then said, "Anyone, poor or not, should at least have enough self-respect, not to mention consideration for others, to bathe regularly. I'll *buy* you some soap if you have none; and I know that there's at least a washtub or something else suitable around your house in which you could bathe yourself."

These humiliating words did not seem to bother Rita Jean. "I just wasn't raised to bother myself with bathing, Miss Edwards," she replied. "Besides, my momma says that it's good to keep the earth on you. She says that the earth on you helps you tune in better to the proper powers."

"What do you mean, 'proper powers'?" demanded the teacher.

"Well, it's kind of hard to explain," answered the girl. "I guess you could say that I'm talking about some real old kind of things that have been floating around in a different dimension for millions and millions of years watching and waiting. Real old things that you can get to do stuff for you if you get tuned into them all right. I guess they're kind of like them old god kind of things that that man Lovecraft liked to write about. They're real powerful, too, and—"

"That's enough!" cried Miss Edwards. "I've never heard such perverted, blasphemous talk. I see that your mouth needs soap just as much as your body. Well, young lady, I *am* going to have a talk with your mother."

"I don't know if that would be such a good idea, Miss Edwards. My momma doesn't care for it when folks start poking around in our own business."

"When one of my students refuses to practice proper hygiene, it becomes *my* business!" exclaimed Miss Edwards. "I'm going to have a talk with your mother this very afternoon after school, Rita Jean—

about these strange and filthy ideas in your mind as well as about the dirt and filth on your body."

And Miss Edwards was true to her word. After school that day, she drove out to see Rita Jean's momma. But as Rita Jean had claimed, her momma didn't appreciate nosey people poking around in her business. And "old lady Shumate" was quite an enlightened, powerful woman.

The following morning, Miss Edwards didn't seem quite the same. She didn't seem the same ever afterward for that matter. Maybe visiting with Rita Jean's momma wasn't such a good idea after all; for from that day onward, Miss Edwards seemed frightened, even cowed. Maybe Miss Edwards had meddled in something that mortals, at least the ordinary ones, should avoid. Something not natural, and, perhaps, very powerful. Something, perhaps, as Rita Jean had claimed, watches and waits. Whatever it was, she had certainly come away the worse for it. And she never reproached Rita Jean about her lack of hygiene anymore. From that day on, she didn't bother her about anything.

But Jerry Thrash and the rest of the class did. Now, Jerry Thrash was the class clown. It seems that every classroom in every school has a Jerry Thrash—the kind of kid who loves to act silly and make the girls laugh. Yes, Jerry Thrash loved to joke and clown; and he found in Rita Jean Shumate an unlimited source of inspiration for his juvenile antics and wit.

"Hey you, cootie girl," he would taunt. "How many cooties have hatched out on you today?" And the other boys and girls would snicker. Or he would ask, "Hey, you, Rita Germs, how did you get allergic to soap and water?" And the class would laugh again. As for Rita Jean, she would not respond at all. She remained quiet and tried to ignore her persecutors.

One day Jerry came up with an idea, a very mean idea. He decided that the time had finally arrived to take action against Rita Jean's dirty body. And he knew just how to do it.

His plan involved Denten's Country Laundry, an establishment located next to the school. Denten's Country Laundry had initially had problems with the disposal of the waste produced by its machines. There was no sewage line in that part of Webster County to channel away the dirty water and suds, and there was too much of the waste for a conventional septic tank to handle. So, Mr. Denten had decided to just use a large sink hole, always full of water in back of the laundry and adjacent to the school grounds. He simply piped it there; and, upon receiving no complaints from the authorities or anyone else, he considered his problem solved.

All the kids at school knew about the sink hole of course, including Jerry Thrash; and it was in there that he decided he would "help" Rita Jean finally take a "bath." Naturally he desired an audience to witness his grand prank, so he passed the word around to his giggling classmates.

"Tomorrow, like it or not, that kid's going to have a bath!" he laughed.

The next day was cold and wet. It was perfect, thought Jerry. The extra misery this meant for his victim would just add to the fun. He couldn't wait for morning recess, the time he intended to act.

When recess finally arrived, the conspirators, led by Jerry, approached Rita Jean. Jerry did the talking.

"Hey, Rita Jean, have you been down to the sink hole lately? There's something weird down there. There's some kind of animal's nest with strange looking babies in it."

"Really?" the victim asked.

"Yeah!" replied Jerry. "Come on down there with us to see them so you can tell us if you know what kind of animals they are."

And so Rita Jean went to the sink hole with the rest of the class.

"Well, where are the weird animal babies?" she asked.

"Actually, there are none," said Jerry. "You see, we've been thinking real hard about you lately, Rita Germs. We've been thinking how much better and cleaner you'd feel if you took a bath and got them cooties off you."

Rita Jean did not reply right away. For a few moments she just looked at Jerry and the rest of the kids. Then she said, "Like I told

Miss Edwards, my momma says that it's good to keep the earth on you as much as you can."

"Well, your momma's wrong!" Jerry shouted. "And now you're finally going to get good and wet and sudsy! It's time we got rid of all those cooties you got before you spread them around to everybody!"

And with that, he pushed her into the freezing, filthy water with the dirty suds. Rita Jean screamed, and then struggled to get out. But she slipped and fell back in. And meanwhile, all the other kids laughed and taunted.

"Hey, Rita Germs," cried Jerry, "you wash yourself real good now! Put them suds all over you and wash off all those millions of cooties you got!"

All the other kids kept watching her, laughing loudly as she continued trying to escape the sink hole. Finally she secured her footing and slowly crept out, shivering and crying. She made her way back to the school house to get a towel and dry off. And as she walked away, she heard Jerry shouting behind her.

"You'd better start taking real baths now, Rita Germs, or we'll throw you in here again!"

After school that day, Rita Jean had a little talk with her momma. And old lady Shumate—you could ask Miss Edwards—was a very strange, scary and, let us say, "learned" woman.

* * *

A week later, it was time for "show and tell." Usually this is a pretty boring activity; and the talking and demonstrating today in Miss Edward's classroom was, thus far, no exception. It seemed that no one captured anyone's interest in what he or she had to demonstrate about. But when Rita Jean's turn came around, the class livened up immediately.

Standing before them, she began. "Today I'm going to show you something that my momma taught me to do."

"Hey, Rita Germs!" It was Jerry Thrash, of course, interrupting her. "Why don't you show us your cooties and talk about them!"

And all the boys and girls burst out laughing.

"Cootie girl, cootie girl, cootie girl!" Jerry stood up and motioned for the rest of the kids to join in his chanting. Miss Edwards, meanwhile, did nothing. Ever since her visit with Rita Jean's momma, she had more or less relinquished control of the classroom to the students.

"Cootie girl, cootie girl, cootie girl!" The whole class was chanting it now. And Jerry Thrash was standing on his desk chair leading them in the chant with his arms like an orchestra conductor.

"I SAID THAT TODAY I'M GOING TO SHOW YOU SOMETHING THAT MY MOMMA TAUGHT ME TO DO."

And now the class was silent. During that outburst, Rita Jean's voice had boomed out like she spoke through a powerful, public address system. Then, speaking again in her regular voice, she continued.

"You see, my momma knows lots of good tricks, and she taught me how to perform one the other day. You entities think I've got cooties, huh? Well, today I'm going to show you some *real* cooties. Lots of real cooties."

Rita Jean paused for a few moments, smiling. Then she started turning her body slowly in a counterclockwise direction and moving her arms in very strange gestures. Next, she recited an odd little verse:

"Oh, great yellow cloudy one, oh, great Goth-lee-geed,
Gather, now, thyself above us, bloated with thy seed!"

And, as if in immediate answer to Rita Jean's command, the room grew dark. It was as if twilight had settled in prematurely. Something was casting a very dark shadow over the school building. This caused all the kids to look around at each other with fearful expressions on their faces.

Then Rita Jean starting reciting again:

"Oh, great breath of Nex-hoth, I ask of thee thy strength,
Split this ceiling asunder, and uncover us at length."

And again little Rita Jean's command was apparently to be answered. For now the wind began to blow. At first there was just a small breeze; but it quickly grew stronger and stronger as the little spell-caster continued turning and gesturing. Soon there was a regular hurricane; and it was pulling at the roof. Everyone could hear the rafters creaking and groaning, and they were terrified. Then the storm tore the roof completely off, revealing a gigantic, sickly yellow cloud hovering above.

And she continued chanting. The vicious wind was howling all around in the room, but she was the only one who did not seem to need to struggle to keep her feet.

> *"Spawn of the mighty, though men call ye vile,*
> *Come thickly down upon us, O plague of the Nile."*

And then the wind died; but things began falling from the cloud. They were tiny yellow squirming things. Rita Jean had called them "cooties," but actually they were more like maggots. At first they fell very lightly; and when all the boys and girls realized the nature of the things that were now landing on them, they, filled with revulsion, frantically started brushing them off. But their efforts were futile, for now the things fell more heavily, causing the kids to scream in terror and disgust. The classroom was now filled with an odious, suffocating stench from the creatures. But these things did more than merely stink: they also stung...and bit. And the kids screamed in torment. Soon the things were pouring down in sheets, forming a quickly rising layer on the floor. It was becoming difficult to see through them...and breathe.

"Hundreds of cooties and thousands of cooties and millions of cooties!" screamed Rita Jean. They were falling on her also, but she didn't mind at all. On the contrary, she enjoyed the loathsome shower. She held out her arms to them as if enjoying a refreshing rainfall following a long drought. She did this as she, laughing, floated around the room.

The writhing carpet was rising very fast now, and some of the kids were climbing on their desks trying to keep above it. Others tried stepping and pressing their way through the squirming mass to the door; for that was the only exit; for the windows were secured from entry or exit with burglar bars. But Rita Jean spoiled this. With a flick of her wrist, she locked it before any could escape.

And still the cooties, or maggots, or whatever they were, rained down from the yellow cloud. They came down in absolute torrents now, and were piling high enough to go for ears and nostrils and mouths. The kids were still screaming, when they weren't gagging, but it was Jerry Thrash who now occupied Rita Jean's attention. He was frantically trying to wipe them away from his nose, and spitting them out of his mouth. But it was to no avail, for the squirming little things just kept rising higher. It was like living, writhing quicksand coming up to suffocate him. Every time he opened his mouth to take in air, they poured in.

"Why aren't you laughing now?" Rita Jean asked him. "I guess *real* cooties don't make a very funny joke, do they?"

And then she watched them close completely over his head, muffling the sound of his gagging and choking.

Finally, she floated over to Miss Edwards, who, being the tall woman she was—and who also stood on her desk—was the last person, besides Rita Jean, who could still breathe. The girl then made a certain motion with her right arm and the things stopped falling.

"I don't suppose you'll be giving anymore homework," the girl said, "but it doesn't matter, because there's nobody left to give any homework to. As for me, I'm leaving school for good. You see, the stuff I can learn at home is much better than school learning. My momma and I have decided to start having our own way around this county; and if the people don't like it, it'll be the worse for them. They had *better* like it, or we'll gross them out real good too—gross them out dead!"

And then Rita Jean floated up and away over the school house. She was going home to have another little talk with her momma.

PROFESSOR PATCHWHITE'S GARDEN

If there ever really existed a man who could truly boast that he was indeed God's gift to women, then it was Ron Gregg. Ron Gregg was an extremely good-looking guy. He almost looked too good to be real. The noble bone structure of his face was a great pleasure in the eyes of any girl who saw it. Everything was pleasing about his face. He possessed enormous blue eyes that would almost cause any lady who peered into them to swoon. And his handsome, classical shaped nose, his stately shaped mouth and his noble, strong chin were the envy of any male. Everything was complemented by his thick, shiny blond hair, which he always brushed back in a pompadour. And his body was just as magnificent as his countenance. From his broad shoulders and tapering torso to his bulging thighs and calves, he was completely irresistible to the female eye. And the muscles in his legs were not the only things that bulged. It was obvious, from his tight jeans that he was resplendent down below.

Yes, he was completely, he was overwhelmingly attractive to the girls. And they were all the time "accidentally" brushing up against him to feel, if only for a moment, his body against their own.

And if this was not enough an advantage for him, he was also very wealthy and due to inherit his dad's executive position in the local furniture factory. And he certainly flaunted his affluence. He wore the finest clothes one could buy. He had them tailored to fit his splendid physique. He wore the finest footwear available and the most expensive watches on his wrist. And he possessed plenty of costly toys—including a midnight blue corvette and a flaming red jaguar.

He was young, handsome and rich. He had everything going his way. But the problem was in his personality. It was absolutely shitty. His looks and wealth had ballooned the size of his head. His ego loomed like the Sears Tower in Chicago. He was completely consumed with himself. He loved to stand naked in front of full-length mirrors for long lengths of time and simply admire his body, reveling in the size of his manhood. He took great pride in the fact that if he had lived in Nazi Germany, he would definitely have qualified as a supreme example of the Nordic "new man." He would have been Hitler's pride and joy. And his philosophy, by the way, would have fit right in with that historical aberration's way of thinking.

As was mentioned, getting women was no problem at all with him. The fact that he could have any girl he wanted was almost as sweet to him as the actual sex itself. Especially did he delight in stealing girls away from their boyfriends. And if any of the guys tried to physically object to this, his black belt karate skill always carried him safely through. Indeed, he had bloodied up more than a few dudes in his time, and he thoroughly enjoyed meting out the punishment.

Now this asshole was a college man, a senior at Mississippi State University. So he was around all of the pretty college girls he might want to screw. Penelope Patchwhite was also involved with the university. But Penelope Patchwhite was not a giggling college girl easily infatuated with good looks. No, she was an instructor, a horticulture professor. She was very intelligent; and she definitely knew her flora. She seemed to know everything there was to know about plants. But this was not what impressed Ron about her. He was too shallow to be impressed by female intellect. Rather it was her looks that did it for him. She was a complete knockout. Just gazing at her caused the blood to rush down below. She had a delicate, almost feline way of moving her slender body around that drove him crazy. And he could not help studying her face. Yes, it is clichéd to state she possessed the face of a goddess, but, nevertheless, this was true. It appeared, more or less, Anglo-Saxon, but there was something else about it. Something exotic. Something East Indian, or Oriental about it that overwhelmed him. He resolved that he had to have her.

Nor was it long before he made his move. One afternoon after her class, Ron stayed behind. He waited until everyone had left, then he approached her desk.

"You sure do know a lot about plants, don't you, Professor Patchwhite?" He was ridiculously confident.

"Why, thank you, Ron," she replied. "But it's only my business to know them. It's a wonderful arrangement between us and them, don't you think? We breathe in oxygen and release carbon dioxide; they take in carbon dioxide and, through photosynthesis, release oxygen. And they make for excellent nutrition—not to mention pleasing decoration. What would we do without them?"

"Yes, plants are certainly important," Ron admitted. "But you can't say they are the greatest things in the world." And he gave her a hungry, wry smile.

"No, I don't suppose you could, Ron. But, could you give me an example of something better?" He was completely transparent to her.

"Love, Professor, love. You know, people getting together. I mean good no strings sex."

"Maybe you have a point there," replied the professor. Of course he did not discern it, but she was laughing uproariously inside her mind at him.

"Sure I do." And then he became presumptive and crude. "I've seen you looking at me during you lectures. I think you want me pretty badly."

"You *are* a fairly attractive person, I will admit," replied Professor Patchwhite. "And you're right. I have studied you over from time to time."

"Of course you have," replied the egotistical jerk. "So what do you say me and you get it on together real soon?"

Professor Patchwhite didn't hesitate. "An excellent idea! What about tonight? We'll have supper together—and get stoned. I'll show you my garden. And then…."

"Yeah, and then?"

We'll see." And the professor smiled.

"Oh, man!" cried Ron. "I can't wait!"

Professor Patchwhite had just let him in her house; and he was expressing his surprise and delight at all of the flora in the living room. He had never seen so many house plants in a room before. And they were all huge; they seemed to sprawl everywhere—the tendrils crawling out of the pots all the way to the floor. And the room was completely suffused with the perfume the plants emitted. It was so sweet and overwhelming, that he almost felt intoxicated. Ron guessed that most were exotic. But aside from a lush, magnificent Venus-fly-trap—the species of which, incidentally, was carnivorous—he recognized none of them.

"Do you like my plants?" asked his host.

"Yeah, they're all right. As far as plants go, I guess I like 'em fine. They sure caught me by surprise, though. I've never seen so many in one crib before. And they sure are weird looking. What kind of a plant is this?"

He was pointing at a huge yellowish green bulb or vegetable blob protruding up out of a large vase. Extending out from it all around were long, thick, almost cephalopod like tendrils. And as he looked, he could swear that one of the tentacle looking vines twitched.

"You mean George. Yes, George is really something, isn't he? *Viridis diabolus* is the species. He's a very rare specimen, indeed—and quite carnivorous. I ordered him from Brazil. He comes from the rain forest.

"He sure is ugly," Ron observed. "He kind of looks like an octopus. What does he eat? Kittens and puppies?"

Professor Patchwhite did not answer him. Instead she asked, "Well, now, how about something to eat?"

"Sure," he laughed. "It's always good to energize yourself before you get it on with some chick."

Without joining in his chortle, his hostess disappeared into the kitchen. Five minutes later, she emerged from there carrying a large steaming bowl of something. She set the bowl down on the dining room table and dug out of it a green, stringy, fleshy looking lump of some strange substance. She put it in his plate, then handed him some bread and a beer. Next, she dished out another portion of the unappealing looking stuff for herself. After seating herself at the table with him, she very heartily began to eat the strange food.

"What the hell is this?" he asked with a frown.

"It's called manch," replied the professor. It's a new strain of vegetable, a mutant I cultivated myself. I also named it. Go ahead; eat up. It's very good. Good for you, too."

"Mine looks kind of like a hand, a big green hand," Ron observed. "I don't know if I really..."

"Oh, go ahead." There was a slight hint of command in her voice. "Eat up. It won't hurt you."

"Well, okay. But this better be good. I wouldn't touch it if I weren't starving."

And with that, he took a bite. He chewed it for a while; then, with mouth full, he exclaimed, "Hey, this ain't bad. It tastes lush and sweet—like it's got lots of minerals or something in it."

"I knew you would like it," responded the professor. "I always feed my male visitors my manch. I value their feedback on the quality of its taste."

They continued with supper, then upon finishing the meal, Ron bluntly ventured, "Well, Prof, what do you say about us getting it on now?"

"Why don't I get you high and then let you see my greenhouse first?" suggested the hostess. And she reached in her purse and pulled out a joint. "I love to get guys stoned and show them my garden. I want you to see what manch looks like when it's growing." And she lit the joint and handed it to her guest.

"Here," she said. "Try this out."

"Alright!" cried Ron. And he snatched it out of her hand. He greedily sucked the smoke in, then exhaled with a satisfied sigh. He inhaled and exhaled it again and again, not offering her any of it. Then, when it was all gone—and with a stupid looking smile on his face—he exclaimed, "Whooee! Lady, you sure know your weed!"

"Thank you," she answered. "Now, come with me to my garden."

"Sure thing, baby. Let's go get it on in your garden!" And he started laughing idiotically. He attempted to rise from his chair, but still giggling, collapsed back in it. "Whooee! Give me some seeds of this stuff. I gotta grow some for myself!"

"Here, give me your hand," said the professor.

"I'd rather give you something else!" And he snickered like a little kid.

"Give me your hand!" commanded Professor Patchwhite.

He did as he was told—and was almost snatched out of the chair.

"Whoa! Take it easy, lady. That stuff made me dizzy as shit!"

"Come on, fool! I want you in my garden!"

She half led him, half drug him outside and into the greenhouse. Babbling stupidly, Ron felt as though he were floating in the clouds. But when he saw what grew in the greenhouse—and smelled the air—he gasped and crashed back down to earth.

In the greenhouse, he saw rows of large silver garbage cans. Sticking up out of each can were long, sturdy poles. And tied to the poles in the cans were certain curious things. Things that resembled human male bodies. They were green, fleshy and frightfully misshapen. Some possessed lumpy, stringy appendages, some did not. Some had deformed, rudimentary faces; some had no faces at all. And they stank. The smell assailing his nose was like the escaping stench of a load of vegetables confined in a newly opened freezer that had been without power for days. It was so powerful and rancid that he gagged.

"Straighten up there!" shouted the professor, who was now suddenly wielding a whip. "Straighten up!" And she began to use it on the hideous things. In response to her lashes, they began writhing on the poles and making hissing sounds.

"Well, what do you think of my little crop of manch?" she inquired of her shocked visitor.

Ron did not answer. He just stood there with mouth and eyes wide open in disbelief at the horrid things growing in the cans. They seemed to blaspheme creation itself.

Professor Patchwhite beamed with pride as she continued. "They are my main source of joy. I love growing them, I love showing them off and I love eating them."

It took several moments before Ron could compose himself to say anything. But finally he managed to ask, "But what in the world are they?"

"I told you. They are manch."

"But what kind of seeds do they come from?"

"Not exactly 'seeds,'" she responded. "More properly, 'parts.' I take the parts I need to grow them from both strangers and acquaintances. You know, salesmen, guys pushing their religion, or the real creeps, men like you, who are only out for a piece of ass. They furnish the parts I need, and I plant them. Then, with the special fertilizer I've developed, the manch shoots up in almost no time."

The professor now paused for a few moments. She was looking Ron over.

Then she slyly ventured, "And I think you'll make a very nice specimen. Yes, I'll grow *you* next. And don't think you won't know it. Yes, you'll be aware—tied to your pole. For, you see, growing manch is rather like cloning. It's rather like recreating your body *and* your awareness."

"Man, you're crazy, lady!" cried Ron. And he started to back out of the greenhouse. But he found this very difficult; for the marijuana, or whatever the substance was that she had given him, still asserted itself; he found moving almost impossible.

"George!" called out the professor.

And Ron soon heard a loud, swishing sound behind him. Before he could turn to perceive the source of the noise, he was engulfed by several vines or tentacles. It was George come to grab him.

The plant had uprooted itself in response to its mistress's summons and had him pinioned.

"Now, before I permit George to play with you, I'll just relieve you of the parts I need to grow you," said merry Professor Patchwhite, now brandishing an old timey barber's razor. She uttered nothing more. She just undid his jeans and reached for his testicles.

COUSIN PETE'S ARMADILLO FARM

Randy Tyler suddenly realized that he was probably one of the most miserable men alive. It had to be at least a hundred degrees, the air conditioner in the old Impala was out, he was badly sunburned, and he detested the passenger riding with him. Yeah, that was what she was now, just a passenger. And he was going to see a lawyer about divorcing her just as soon as they returned to Atlanta. He had finally had enough of Doris. The trip to the Grand Canyon—which had been a last attempt to save their marriage—had only made things worse. It had only helped him to realize at last what a true bitch she really was. All she had done on this trip was complain. She had complained about his choice of restaurants, his choice of motels, his driving, and even his eroding prowess in bed. She had even complained about the Grand Canyon itself. "It's not so great," she had bitched. "It's just a big hole in the ground with water running through the bottom of it." And, as usual, she had continued her habit of pestering him. "Take the scenic route home, Randy. I want to see all the small towns and stuff." That was why, instead of zooming their way back home on the interstate, they were now practically creeping along on an ancient, God forsaken two lane highway somewhere in west Texas.

"Uhhh! There's another one," said Randy. And, in spite of the treacherous bumpy road, he pushed down on the accelerator and steered the car straight at something crossing the highway. With perverse satisfaction he enjoyed the sound and feel of the two thumps under the car as he ran over it. With even more pleasure he checked his rearview mirror and looked at what he had hit writhing and dying on the asphalt. It was an armadillo. Not the first he had run over, either. They were all over west Texas; and Randy just didn't like them. He considered them as nasty, mutant looking creatures that had no place on the planet. Their rodent looking heads disgusted him—along with their ugly little feet and nude shingled tails. He hated their gray banded shells too—and especially the hair that stuck out from under it. And what in the hell was a *mammal* doing with a shell on it anyway! He figured that they should have lived with the dinosaurs—and gone out with them. He really detested them; and the fact that his Uncle Bert had once warned him about them made them even more loathsome to him. "Don't ever mess with them things, boy," he had warned. "Don't ever touch one, alive or dead. They carry..." What was it? He couldn't remember. All he knew was that his uncle had mentioned some kind of dreadful disease. Anyway, he had always heeded Uncle Bert's advice. He had never touched one, and never intended to.

"You sicko creep!" cried Doris. "That's the third one you've hit. What's with you?"

"I don't like 'em," Randy answered. "They're nasty little bastards."

That was the last words they spoke to each other for an hour. They simply had nothing to say to each other. Then, Randy broke the silence, "Oh Christ, that's all I need!"

He was reacting to the sight of an old weather-beaten sign coming up on the right. It read, "Food and gas five miles ahead at Cousin Pete's Armadillo Farm."

"Do you think it's still open?" inquired Doris.

"It doesn't matter," Randy replied. "We've got plenty of gas and I'm not hungry."

"*You're* not hungry!" snapped his passenger. "You don't even consider me!"

"There's sandwiches on the back seat."

"Not food, you jerk. I need a restroom."

Randy took a deep breath and exhaled it tightly through his lips. "Okay. We'll stop if it's open." The truth was that he had to go pretty badly also, but would have much preferred the brush instead of an armadillo farm.

A few minutes later, they turned into the place the sign had advertised. It was an old broken-down structure, made of adobe brick, which appeared to have once served as both a restaurant and residence. It was a depressing scene. Garbage was scattered everywhere, and overall was a disagreeable odor. It smelled like the monkey house in a zoo.

"Oh, this is beautiful!" exclaimed the driver. "Great idea, sweetheart!"

"Just shut up!"

Randy, considering the place deserted, was about to back out of the parking lot. But then somebody opened the door of the building and strolled out toward them. This person seemed to be a stranger to hygiene even from a distance; but when he was close enough for them to smell, they found him downright repulsive. He was a tall, skinny old man whose head was wrapped up in a bright red paisley bandana and was crowned with a wide brimmed straw hat. His face seemed to be nothing but wrinkles—wrinkles and ugly white splotches and nodules. His teeth were missing, as well as part of his nose. He was clothed in a long-sleeved gray flannel shirt, faded around the armpits, and a pair of pin-striped overalls. Down below were suede boots caked with mud. Yes, he was quite an unwholesome looking character—and also intimidating. For he also sported a forty-five caliber pistol on his hip.

"How yuh doin,' folks? I'm Cousin Pete. What can I do for ye?" His voice was almost falsetto, and his breath could make one gag.

Doris answered him. "Well, we were hoping we could use your restrooms."

"Shore yuh can, shore yuh can. That's one of the reasons I'm here. Ain't good fer folks to carry piss around inside 'em fer too long a time, is it?"

"Ha ha, no it's not," Randy chuckled. And he gave Doris a look that asked, *"What kind of fucker is this!"*

"Well, come on in and relieve yourselves and visit with me," said Cousin Pete. "I hardly ever git company."

They got out of the car and followed the old man into the restaurant, which turned out to be just as repellent as the proprietor. The zoo smell was even worse inside, and dust, grime and spider webs covered everything. Everywhere there were flies—the fat green kind—and they were busy visiting scattered piles of excrement on the floor.

"You'll just have to excuse all the shit in here," advised Cousin Pete. "It's from my pets. I let 'em in here a lot. In there are the restrooms." He motioned the direction with his left hand, and Randy noticed that, like part of his nose, two of his fingers were missing.

The pent-up stench of the restroom almost floored Randy when he opened the door. The room reeked of unflushed urine and stool. It was so nauseous that he pulled his shirt up to his nose, attempting to filter it out. The seat was down, and to avoid touching it with his hand, he used his foot to lift it. Then, as he relieved himself, he wondered why he had even bothered. He chuckled, because he knew that in the next room, Doris, who had rushed to the john ahead of him, had to be more careful than he did to avoid touching the commode. After all, she had to actually squat over the thing. He had a full load. He seemed to piss forever; then, without bothering to flush the bowl, he opened the door, wanting to get out of this stinking building as soon as possible.

Oh, give me a break, you stupid cunt!

Back in the main room, he found Doris, who had somehow finished ahead of him, if she had bothered to go at all, questioning this filthy character about his nasty establishment. He knew she was doing it just to spite him.

"Yeah, the interstate ruined me," said the old man. "This used to be the main stretch, and I had a good thing goin' fer me. All kinds of people would stop by fer gas and eats; and when they were through eatin,' I'd take 'em outside and show off my 'dillers to 'em. But that was years and years ago."

"But you still raise armadillos?" Doris inquired.

"Yes, ma'am," responded Cousin Pete. "Heh heh, you see the evidence there on the floor. I still raise 'em—and breed 'em too. And the good thing 'bout havin' so much free time now, is that I git to pay more attention to 'em. I been doin' lots of experimentin' through the years with 'em. I been cross breedin' 'em with other things. I even used a little magic with 'em. Heh heh, the devil's magic, yuh might say. They're my pride and joy. And I got 'em trained too. I can make 'em do stuff that would amaze yuh. Do you want to see 'em do some tricks?"

"No, I'm afraid not," Randy broke in. "Doris, we've got to be going now." The last thing in the world he desired to experience at that moment was a trained armadillo show.

"Excuse my dear husband's lack of enthusiasm," Doris remarked. "But he doesn't care much for armadillos. Why, just today he purposely ran over three on the road."

"Oh, yeah?" Cousin Pete smiled. "Well, I got a feelin' he'll like the new crop I reared up. These new 'dillers are something else, I tell yuh. They're smart and spunky and mind me sure 'nuff. So y'all stay and watch the show."

"Maybe next time," said Randy. "Come on, Doris, let's go."

"Well, then, I guess I'll just have to *insist* yuh stay." Cousin Pete smiled again, and slowly pulled out the pistol and began to fondle it. "It seems that folks nowadays are all rush rush rush. And that's just too bad. Like I said, sometimes yuh just have to *insist* to people that they slow down and enjoy themselves." And he pointed the gun right at Randy.

The couple said nothing. They could only look at each other and then back to the old man, their mouths open with surprise at this sinister turn of events.

"Now, before I start the show, I want to know yore names. I like to know my audience personally."

His audience looked at each other again, but did not answer right away. As yet, they really couldn't. They were too stunned—and too frightened.

"Now, am I gonna have to *insist* again?" And Cousin Pete cocked the revolver.

"Tyler—Randy and Doris Tyler." Randy got it out quickly in a shaky voice.

"Well, Randy, nice to know you and Doris. I git the feelin' that you two don't quite care fer each other. That's a shame. You need to enjoy something good together. Something like my 'dillers. So just sit right down in them seats there and git comfortable. Meanwhile, I'll git 'em in here."

After the scared couple obeyed him, Cousin Pete walked to a door by the dusty counter and opened it.

"Chillin,' git in here!"

And immediately a troop of the most repulsive things that Randy and Doris had ever seen rushed into the diner. In a way they resembled normal armadillos, but they were some kind of nightmare breed. They were much larger than average armadillos. They were the size of fat sows. Their shells were a dull, greenish-gray color, and were covered with some sort of thorny projections. Long brown straw like hair stuck out from under it. Their heads resembled rat's heads—the salivating mouths flashing long, canine fangs. Their frightful tails were scaly and reticulated. But maybe the most disagreeable feature about them were their hairy limbs, the paws of which resembled those of monkeys—and which were equipped with long claws that clicked on the floor as the creatures scampered toward Randy and Doris.

"Hold up there!" shouted the old man. And the things halted in front of the terrified couple. There were six of them in all, and their wicked looking red eyes were glued on the two people sitting before them, their mouths drooling.

"Well, what do yuh think of my 'dillers?" asked the proud old man.

"They're...nice," Doris managed to answer. She was scared to death.

"Just wait'll yuh see 'em do the tricks I taught 'em!" beamed Cousin Pete. "Alright, chillin, y'all ready?"

The creatures hissed and snorted.

"Okay! Ladies and gentlemen, welcome to the show!" For the first trick, my 'dillers will piss on command…on you!" He paused, then commanded, "Do it, chillin!"

And immediately the armadillos, or whatever they were, sprang forward toward Randy and Doris and did it on their legs. The couple watched in horrified silence, then quickly felt the hot liquid soaking through their jeans onto their skin. And meanwhile, Cousin Pete, who must have thought it very amusing, laughed.

Then he became serious again. "And now, fer the next trick, I'll command Franky to git his rocks off." He peered lecherously at Doris. "Hunch 'er leg, Franky!"

And at this, one of the beasts, it must have been Franky, reared up and grabbed the girl's leg like a horny dog and vigorously obeyed his master command. It showed something long, hard and slimy. Doris was absolutely paralyzed with terror and revulsion. All she could do was watch in silence as the thing that was fastened to her leg vigorously pumped it.

Cousin Pete was watching too—and reaching his hand deep inside his overalls. Quickly he breathed very hard; for his hand was very busy in there. It stayed busy for a minute more; then he shouted out, "Whoooooeeee!" and slouched back in his chair. A few moments later, he composed himself and issued another command.

"Okay, Franky, slack off." And the creature obeyed.

"P-please," Doris sobbed. "Please stop this and let us go."

"Aw, what's wrong, Doris? You don't care for my little show? Maybe the next trick will change your mind. Stick out yore pinky."

Doris, pleading and whimpering, slowly put her trembling arm out and extended her little finger.

"Good girl! Now, Charlie, grab holt of that little thing!"

And another creature jumped forward and placed the appendage in its mouth. It had bulging jaw muscles and, as was mentioned, strong, sharp teeth. Doris knew that it could easily bite her finger right off; and she sobbed uncontrollably.

Charlie stood poised, awaiting the old man's command to sever the finger. But Cousin Pete said, "Now don't carry on so, Doris. My 'diller's ain't really that keen to fingers. Let go, Charlie."

And Charlie released the finger.

"Naw, my 'dillers don't like fingers much. They're too boney. They *are* partial to innards though." And he then shouted, "Suppertime, chillin! Go fer them guts!"

And all six of the things leaped on poor Doris, drug her down from her chair and growling and shrieking, tore and bit away at her abdomen. Screaming in pain and terror, she tried to fight them off, but it was hopeless. Shreds of flesh went flying. Quickly they reached the luscious entrails they sought—which they pulled out and fought over. That was the final thing Doris saw before she died.

The grisly feast did not last very long; for Franky and Charlie and the gang were very hungry. They swallowed them guts right down. When the repast was complete, the old pervert started talking again.

"Well, Randy, it looks like you're a widower. I figure you owe me a big thank you for that—seein' as how you probably wanted to be free of ole Doris anyways. But you needn't bother me with yore words of gratitude; just enjoy the rest of the show. And it's time fer the big finale; the star attraction. It's time fer you to meet Momma Gretel. Why do yuh look that way, Randy? You didn't think these were full growed, did yuh? Hell, they're just young 'uns. Now I got Momma Gretel fastened up in that room yonder, and what I want you to do now is go over there and let her out…hey, Momma Gretel!"

And at this, Randy heard a very loud scratching sound behind the door to which Cousin Pete had referred.

"Go on, Randy. Go let 'er out. She likes strangers."

Now it was Randy's turn to whimper and plead. "Please, just let me go. Please."

"Not 'til you've met Momma Gretel. Go on now." And he aimed the revolver right at Randy's face.

So Randy slowly crept toward the door. Upon reaching it, he put a trembling hand on the doorknob. And he heard the scratching inside become more intense. He also heard low growling sounds. He slowly turned the knob, then was knocked to the floor by the door as it flew open. Nor was he able to get up, because he found himself pinned to the floor by the crushing weight of his worst nightmare come true. It resembled the other creatures, except that it was twice as large and stank twice as strong. Its repulsive, monkey paws pressed down hard on his shoulders. Indeed, the massive weight of the thing made it difficult to breathe. Its frightful face was just inches from his own, and yellow spittle dripped down from its hissing, snorting mouth onto his face. Its breath was absolutely fetid; to breathe it was to choke. Randy knew that it was only waiting for the order to finish him off, but Cousin Pete was silent. With the thing poised above him, an eternity seemed to pass. Then he somehow found the strength to speak.

"Please… I'll do anything. For the love of God, get it off me!" he sobbed.

"Aw, what's the matter, boy? You don't care much for Momma Gretel? She could kill yuh, just like that, yuh know; and I'm tempted to go ahead and let 'er do it. But I won't. I guess it's 'cause I sort of like you. I mean, we got something in common. I figure you to be a real bastard like I am. I tell yuh what: You apologize to Momma Gretel fer runnin' over her kin today, and I'll tell 'er to let you up. Do it, boy—right now, or I'll tell 'er to take yore face clean off!"

Randy didn't hesitate. He immediately told Momma Gretel he was sorry for what he did. And he was too terrified to feel the least bit silly about it.

"Now, kiss her."

He obeyed this loathsome order also.

"Okay, that's better. Momma Gretel, let 'im up now."

Cousin Pete waited until Randy was on his feet, and then continued, "Now, Randy, I'm gonna let you go like I said I was, and I don't care who yuh tell about what happened here today. Tell the law if yuh want to, but it won't do no good. Yuh see, the law don't fuck with me. They know better. Besides, they'd probably think *you* killed ole Doris, and git after *you.* So I 'spect you'll keep yore mouth shut. Now, make tracks real quick outta here, boy, before I change my mind and give you over to Momma Gretel fer good. And I don't think you'll be fergitten' about ole Cousin Pete's Armadillo Farm for a long time."

Six months later, back in Atlanta, Randy, though troubled with nightmares about his terrible experience in Texas, was beginning to feel a little better. He could never forget about such an ordeal, of course, but there was actually something good that had resulted from it. At least he was rid of Doris. And as for Cousin Pete, he resolved not to report the old man to the police. He could just imagine their skeptical faces if he reported the story. *Giant, trained armadillos had killed his wife!*—yeah, right. Besides, he really did not want to become involved with the authorities anyway; and as far as the justice that should be served for Doris's sake, he didn't care. So he just let it ride—and told his wife's family and friends that the two of them, realizing that they could no longer abide each other, went to Mexico while out west and had their marriage annulled. And Doris, he lied, falling in love with Phoenix, Arizona, had decided to remain there indefinitely. Nor did he need to tell many people this fabrication anyway, because she had hardly any family and few friends, the bitch.

Yeah, everything had actually sort of happened for the best. He was free of Doris—and without having to spend money on divorce lawyers and alimony. Yeah, things were looking up. But if only those white splotches on his body would go away—and those things on his face. What were they—some sort of big pimples or nodules or something? And also, some of his fingers now felt numb all the time. And they had a faint, but disagreeable odor about them. This led him, one night, to take a needle and prick one of the affected fingers to check the feeling in it. He felt very little pain. He pushed the needle in deeper. Still minimal pain. And very little blood. He wondered, with horror, if he, with little pain or blood, could press it in all the way to the bone! Then he started to wonder if he had picked up something from those armadillo creatures in Texas. He remembered Uncle Bert's warning all those years ago, concerning these animals:

"Don't ever mess with them things, boy. Don't ever touch one, alive or dead. They carry...."

What *was* it? What had his uncle warned him about? His mind returned to Cousin Pete. He recalled the same kind of splotches and nodules on the old man's face. He also remembered the remains of the nose half rotted away, and the missing fingers. Then, for some reason, the Bible entered his mind—and a dread disease it often mentioned. And it was then that he remembered the rest of what Uncle Bert had said. He was crushed. He wished he were dead. He remembered.

"—they carry leprosy."

REBECCA'S HAND

"Women! How wicked you are in God's sight! How vile! How vindictive! But God will forgive you—so long as you know your place in this world and keep to it!"

It was a sweltering summer night in Appalachia, and the preacher man, one Ezra Stone, was talking it up mightily to his congregation. His church was called "The Tabernacle of the Savior"—one of the two small West Virginia churches on Bald Top Mountain. His listeners considered themselves righteous and penitent, true believers of the faith. True, they did not handle serpents and drink strychnine like the people of "Blessed Souls' Temple"—the church on the other side of Bald Top. But, nevertheless, they were still confident that when their time to live expired, they would rise up to be with the Lord in glory.

And they were proud of their preacher, none more so than the minister's lovely young wife, Rebecca. She was hardly more than a child. Just seventeen, she was young enough to be his daughter. And that was how he treated her. But she loved him, and she smiled with pride as he continued the sermon.

"Yes, women, keep your place and continue to pray to God to keep you from leading your men astray. For, remember, it was *your* kind that caused the downfall of men. Yes, you have always been the ruin of men—ever since Eve gave Adam the forbidden fruit. And do you not remember Delilah, and how she betrayed Samson? How about the wickedness of Jezebel? Do you not recall how she caused the men of Israel to do sinful deeds in the eyes of the Lord? And how about that witch, Athaliah, queen of Judah—who set out to do no less than to end the line of David! Women! Never forget how evil you are! Pray that the Lord does not curse you! Pray that He will not damn you to hell! Remain submissive to your husbands, for surely men are more precious in the eyes of God than you!"

The organ now chimed in climaxing the service. Everyone was clapping, stomping, and shouting. They swayed, they danced, they talked in tongues, they sweated and they raised their arms in supplication and praise. They sang their favorite hymn, "Bringing in the Sheaves," with all the fervor they could muster. Then, when the song concluded, the preacher man led them in a final prayer, thus ending the revival meeting.

"Nice sermon, Preacher," commented Abigail Tribley, the old widow woman, as she passed out of the church. As usual, she was the last of the devout to leave the sanctuary, leaving Ezra and Rebecca alone to secure the building for the night. After extinguishing the lights and locking the door, the Stones, with the evening's tithing in hand, departed the church and headed for their old Ford pickup parked over by the cemetery.

They were just about to enter the vehicle when a shadowy figure appeared from behind a hemlock tree and yelled, "Hey, Preacher, hold up there! I wanna talk to yuh!" As this person approached the truck, Ezra recognized him as Luther Cripe, of the outlaw Cripes who lived down by Lick Creek. He was a very large man and quite ugly—the latter possibly due to the questionable quality of his DNA. Full of moonshine, he staggered up to the couple and abruptly inquired, "Well, Preacher, how much loot did they give yuh tonight?"

Ezra hesitated before responding. He was fairly scared. After all, he knew, as did everybody on Bald Top, that this man had killed before. But he finally responded, "It is the Lord's money, son. And it is not for you to know how much people give Him."

"The hell it ain't! I'm on th' good side of th' Lord too—just like you say *you* are—and I figure I got a right to know. Now why don't you just hand it over to me and let me count it. Besides, heh heh, God told me that tonight all th' money y'all took up in the collection plates was 'sposed to be given to me so's I can fix up my old drafty cabin fer th' winter."

"Now, Luther, why don't you just go on back home? I don't want any trouble from you tonight."

Luther's grin—which had displayed his few remaining, rotten teeth—suddenly went away. Glaring at Ezra, he spat. Then he shouted, "You don't know whut trouble is, Preacher!" Then, without warning, he landed a vicious right uppercut on Ezra's chin.

The preacher stumbled backwards several feet before he regained his balance. Then, realizing that it probably wouldn't be very auspicious to obey the Bible and turn the other cheek, Ezra suddenly charged the drunk with fists flying. His attack caught Luther by surprise, and he was forced back two or three steps. But he was much larger than the preacher, and he quickly retaliated. He soon had Ezra trapped in a deadly choke hold. He shook him violently, all the while shouting obscenities in his captive's face.

Rebecca, meanwhile, was screaming, screaming at the assailant to release her husband. She knew that, unless she took physical action, her husband was in mortal danger. So she jumped on Luther, clawing his face. Luther, however, knocked her to the ground with the back of his hand. Then he resumed his choke hold on Ezra's throat. He meant to choke the life out of him. He was acting on pure, unrestrained rage.

Rebecca looked up at the two. Aghast, she saw her husband's tongue protruding. Her husband was dying. So, on pure instinct, she regained her feet and rushed toward the drunken brute, directing her right hand toward his privates. And her aim was true. She felt the crotch against her palm. And she clenched as hard as she could.

A blood freezing howl burst from Luther's throat. He felt like current from a car battery was shooting up in parallel charges from his genitals up through his stomach all the way to the crown of his head. He immediately released his hold on the preacher and crumpled to the ground bent up like a pretzel. Rebecca had let go by then; so he was free to writhe and roll and scream all he needed to.

The Stones did not linger. After Rebecca had saved her spouse, she helped him to the pickup. He slouched down on the passenger side, coughing and gasping. Rebecca then started the truck and drove away, leaving Luther Cripe still on the ground, writhing and howling with agony.

Ezra Stone acted strangely the next few days. He canceled the remaining nights of the revival, claiming that he was ill. He was oddly quiet, saying hardly anything to his wife. The truth was, the incident with Luther Cripe had left him very pensive and strongly disturbed. The distress over the violent incident with the drunken hillbilly had more or less disappeared; it had diminished along with the marks on his throat. The truth of the matter was that his pride was shaken. It bothered him that a woman, a weak, brainless female, had to preserved his life. And she had done it with one hand, yet. Yes, with her small right hand. And Ezra could not help but fasten his eyes on that appendage whenever Rebecca was around. That *hand*! That weak hand of a woman! He found himself loathing it. Never mind that it had saved his life. Never mind that it belonged to his wife. He could no longer endure the sight of it.

And then it happened that he recalled a passage in the Bible concerning the hands of women. It was a certain piece of scripture written to warn the women of Israel that, in certain circumstances, it was better for them to keep their hands to themselves.

It was Friday night, about two weeks following the experience with Luther Cripe, when Ezra decided to act upon this text. He was waiting at the kitchen table for Rebecca to come home from visiting her Aunt Jenny over in Sassafras Hollow. Upon her arrival, he motioned her to join him at the table. And on this table were three articles: an open Bible, an acetylene torch, and a recently sharpened meat cleaver.

"Sit down, Rebecca," commanded Ezra. "I have something that you need to read."

She obeyed her husband. She sat down facing him.

"Read out loud the verses that are underlined." And he pushed the book over to her.

She looked down at the book. It was turned to the twenty-fifth chapter of the Book of Deuteronomy, with verses eleven through twelve underlined in red ink. She then spoke out the words:

"When men strive together one with another, and the wife of the one draweth near for to deliver her husband out of the hand that smiteth him, and putteth forth her hand and taketh him by his secrets:

"Then thou shalt cut off her hand, thine eye shall not pity her."

Upon reading the verses, Rebecca looked up at Ezra, and what she saw in his face terrified her. Then she saw him grasp the cleaver.

"Now, wife, stretch forth the offending member."

"Ezra! I only did it to save your life!"

"It would have been better for both of us had you stayed the hand." His voice was deliberate, matter of fact. "For then the Lord God would not have been transgressed against. Again I say, stretch forth thy right hand!"

"Ezra!"

"Stretch it forth!"

And Rebecca, sobbing with terror, did as he commanded. She slowly extended her hand across the table.

Nor did Ezra hesitate. He brought the cleaver down on the wrist as hard as he could, and, fortunately, delivered a clean blow. For a few seconds he watched in perverse fascination the severed hand twitching on the table. And his wife's screams were blurred and distant in his ears. Then, shaking off the trance, he grabbed the hemorrhaging arm and lifted it. With his other hand, he grabbed the lit torch and directed the searing flames on the end of the stump, cauterizing the wound. And all the while, poor Rebecca's shrieks seemed to come from a hundred miles away.

Thus Ezra Stone fulfilled his divine duty. Nor did he feel the least bit of guilt or pity for Rebecca. After all, the Good Book forbade it. Providence was avenged. The transgression was set right. But all of this was not actually important to him. The real importance resulting from this business was that his pride was soothed over. Nor would his eyes be tortured any longer by the sight of that hand, either. He had cut it off; and that same night, he buried it out in the backyard.

Rebecca's stump healed well and quickly. True, she had spent the first few days in terrible pain; for her husband had not summoned the doctor. But now, a month after being chastised, the pain was gone, the wrist was healed. At least the physical pain had disappeared. Her mind, however, was anything but at peace. She raged in her spirit. At first, being the faithful, obedient wife that she was supposed to be, she tried to understand and accept the justice of the deed. She attempted to reconcile herself with the fact that Ezra had only obeyed the commands of the Bible, itself. But soon the meek, penitent child within her began to change, began to question the morality of the act. After all, was the Bible, with all of its nebulous, antiquated and oft-times contradicting passages to be taken literally in the present-day world? *Was* it to be taken as the perfect and absolute truth? And what about Christ? Would *He* have approved of her husband's cruel, drastic action? She doubted it. And finally, was not the New Testament supposed to have negated all those strict and cruel laws of the Old Testament anyway? Had not Christ fulfilled the Biblical Law, and thus redeemed mankind from its burden?

With thoughts like these, the subdued little child within her became, secretly, a grown woman thirsting for revenge. Ezra was wrong to have done this to her. And she began to realize what a cruel, shallow man he actually was. He was a monster, a self-righteous bastard. And she began to positively *seethe* inside. She desired vengeance. And she knew just the right person to help her achieve it.

Now, no one living on Bald Top Mountain knew exactly how old Sadie Wick was. It seemed she had been living up on Nebo Mountain, just across from Bald Top, forever. Old Jeremiah Trigg, who was just about the oldest person around those parts, claimed she was already ancient when he was a youth. So, naturally the rumor circulated that she was in league with powers "good Christian folk should not fool around with." Nor did it help her reputation any that she made money selling poisonous snakes to the holy rollers of Blessed Souls' Temple. People claimed she used spells to draw the serpents to her cabin. Yes, folks swore that the reptiles would crawl up to her yard anytime she needed them and placidly allow Sadie Wick to gather them up in burlap sacks. And when the members of Blessed Souls' Temple needed snakes for them to handle and prove their faith, they employed young Josh Hawkins, the local dimwit, to journey up there and purchase them. He was the only one around the community stupid enough to actually ascend Nebo Mountain and conduct business with her.

This was the person that Rebecca decided could help her set things right with Ezra; and so, on the pretext of visiting Aunt Jenny, she left one afternoon to see Sadie Wick.

It was no easy thing to drive the old pickup with only one hand, especially considering that she had to manually shift the thing in the gears, but somehow she managed it. She drove around the crest of Bald Top down past Blessed Souls' Temple. Eventually she reached Sunflower Valley, which separated the two mountains. Upon crossing Pocatock River, she took the right fork of the road, which she knew would end at the foot of Nebo. Arriving there, she found that the road played out. There was only a narrow foot trail in sight. Rebecca parked the truck, and immediately began climbing up.

As she trudged on up, she began to notice a strange quality about the vegetation growing around her. Somehow it seemed too lush, too healthy to be natural. The trees exhibited massive trunks, and towered, it seemed, to the sky. They were so large, in fact, that they conveyed an almost intimidating aspect about them. And then she began to hear the denizens of the forest. Some of the sounds she recognized; some she did not. She discerned the call of the hawk and the crow, but what was causing that strange coughing, grunting noise? And what in the world was making that heavy, crashing, crawling sound? Her ears caught everything, including, now, a whispering ambient roar. She could not tell exactly where it originated. But, nevertheless, it seemed to pervade from everywhere. Her sense of direction started becoming confused. Up and down, right and left became difficult to discern. Very dark, very scary shadows of things she could not discern danced all around her. Time-space itself seemed nebulous, hard to register in the mind. She became dizzy; she became confused. Could the truth be, perhaps, that Nebo Mountain pierced some sort of cosmic void? And was it possible that that mentioned roar, now a cacophonous symphony of wild wails and mocking laughter, was the result of a penetrated metaphysical vortex?

Now, Rebecca was a courageous young woman, but she was now quite terrified. She felt panic welling up within, but she didn't turn back. In spite of the disconcerting sounds and sights, she pressed on. Eventually, she succeeded in reaching the summit and, perceiving Miss Sadie's cabin, breathed a sigh of relief. Although she was fearful of meeting this person, at least she was out of those terrible woods.

Then she saw the door of the cabin slowly open…and there was Sadie Wick herself.

"Come hither, child. Do not turn back now. Come visit with me. Never mind the serpents. They shan't harm you."

And then Rebecca noticed them. They were crawling and slithering all around. The ground was positively alive with serpents. But although they hissed and crawled all around her, they did not touch her.

"Well!" exclaimed the old woman, "your story is one of the vilest tales I've ever heard. Poor child, you did right in coming to see me."

They were sitting at a small, sturdy table in the cabin. Rebecca had just finished relating her story to Sadie Wick. Sadie Wick was angry, and the anger of Sadie Wick was something that *nobody* should want to arouse.

She was tall, lanky and angular, giving all the justice the old granny dress she wore deserved. Her hair was long, unkempt and gray. Yes, very gray—so gray that it seemed almost blue. And it covered her face. About the only thing Rebecca could discern about it was a long pitted nose jutting out through the dirty, mated locks. Oh yes, and the eye. Every now and then Rebecca caught a glimpse of the right eye. And the frightful thing about it was that it seemed to change colors. Sometimes it seemed to be coal black. Other times it appeared livid green. Still other times it portrayed a dingy blue.

"You married a perfect scoundrel, poor child." It was Miss Sadie talking again. "Pride and self is truly Man! Your husband wasn't concerned about any offence to God he claimed you committed. It was his own wounded sense of masculinity that drove him to the dastardly act. Deceiver! He told people that you lost your hand to a bush hog, eh? Well, take comfort, child. He's as good as dead already."

"But I do not wish his death, Miss Sadie. I want a living, lasting revenge."

Rebecca then discerned a few stained teeth within the hair. Miss Sadie must have grinned. Then she spoke again.

"Ah, but you are wise in this matter, young one. For of what benefit is revenge if it merely fleets. What good is vengeance if it is not forever?"

Then the old crone paused for many moments, lost in thought. Then she suddenly jumped up and exclaimed with glee, "Queen of Heaven! Mother of God! I have it. Listen, you claim you know what he did with your hand?"

"Yes, he buried it outside in the yard close to the well."

"Good!"

And with that, the hag walked to a chest of drawers. She grabbed something from the top drawer, again sat down at the table and laid that something down on it. It was a ring, large, shining and exotic. It seemed to shine with a power emanating from within.

Then Sadie Wick spoke again. "You see before you the ring of Athaliah, Queen of Judah. A victim of treason, she was usurped from the throne and slain by cowardly men. This is all that is left of her legacy. But it is a special ring—with wonderful, but dangerous powers. Even I am careful with it."

"But how in the world did you come by it?"

"Child, when one has access to the mighty Akashic Records, one is able to obtain many curious and rare articles. Now, Rebecca, some night when you're ready, dig up your hand and place this ring on the index finger. Then, holding the member aloft towards the three stars comprising the belt of Orion, repeat this incantation." And she spoke out the words of the spell. "Then, Rebecca, when a great blue shaft of light shoots forth into the ring, do not flinch, but hold the hand tight and steady. And when the light ascends back unto the ether, the hand will be your servant."

"It will do as I ask?"

"Child, you will need not utter a word. It will do as your *thoughts* bid." Old Sadie then smiled again. And Rebecca could have sworn that the eye was now a glowing deep crimson color. "Now, I advise you to be off before darkness falls, for nighttime fills old Nebo Mountain with even more mischief."

The following night, while Ezra was away preaching, Rebecca was out in the yard with a trowel digging by the well. To avoid going to church, she had feigned sickness. And she had about an hour to find what she sought. It was fairly obvious where the hand was buried; the ground still appeared disturbed. Nor was the appendage buried very deeply; she soon smelled decay. A moment later, she uncovered the thing. Wasting no time, she placed the ring on the stiff, index finger. Then holding the hand aloft towards the belt of Orion, she recited the words Miss Sadie had quoted to her:

"O Ashtoreth, Great Queen Mother of the Great All, I ask Thee, impart the darker measure of thyself unto this ring so that this severed member that it adorns may do my bidding!"

Then, just as Miss Sadie had foretold, a shaft of blue light shot down from the starry sky and surrounded the hand in a blue aura. And the hand became hot. This surprised Rebecca, but she held on. Then, just as quickly as it had appeared to her, the shaft of light shot upwards back to where it had originated. The hand, meanwhile, had already cooled.

A few moments later, the girl was giggling with delight. She was pleased and happy—because the now lithe fingers of the thing were, at her mental command, wriggling quickly and easily.

"Shed your clothes, wife, and repair to the bed. I feel the must very strongly tonight." This was Ezra's command to Rebecca. He had arrived home from church and wanted some pleasure. It seemed he had never felt so aroused before. He was already discarding his own clothes.

"Yes, husband, I shall. But first, please accept the present I bought for you today. Sit here on the bed while I get it for you."

And Ezra, now completely naked, heeded her request.

"What is the occasion?" he asked.

"Oh, there is not really an occasion," answered Rebecca as she handed him a package. It was an old hat box. "I guess I just wanted to show you how much I appreciate your chastising me for the great sin I committed that night against God and yourself and Luther Cripe. I really think it made me a better person."

"Of course it has!" exclaimed Ezra. He was reaching for the top of the box. "Women are vile, even disgusting! They are a necessary evil. They are full of sin and iniquity, thus they must always be pun—"

The thing he saw in the opened box abruptly stopped Ezra's little sermon. His mouth was open. His eyes were wide. He looked at Rebecca; she was smiling. He looked back down at the smelly, rotten thing in the box. And for the first time in his life, Ezra Stone could think of nothing to say.

But he still could scream. And when the thing suddenly jumped out at him and clutched, that was exactly what he did.

At the next Sunday preaching, Ezra, who was accustomed to wearing only his finest suit to church, shocked his congregation by appearing in overalls. The people didn't know it, but Ezra had a little secret. A little secret only he and his wife—and maybe Sadie Wick—knew about. But if his clothes shocked the congregation, imagine their reaction when, in his sermon, he spoke well of the sex he used to condemn. Why, he actually extolled, actually praised women. He preached about how women, from the beginning of time, had been exploited and abused by men. He seemed nervous as he preached, even frightened. All through the sermon he sweated. And he kept glancing at his wife with fearful expressions. Then he arrived at the conclusion.

"And so listen, my brethren, the Lord desires that you always love, respect and honor your women. For they are the truly blessed ones, the truly loved ones and the truly precious ones in His sight. Always obey them, also, for they are truly…"

Here Ezra stopped. He seemed unable, or unwilling to utter the final word. But suddenly he bent over, grabbed his crotch and screamed. The people stood up, some rushing forward to offer assistance. But Ezra, regaining some composure, waved them off. He looked at Rebecca. She glared at him in way that would freeze water, then nodded for him to finish the sermon.

"As I was saying, men, always obey your women, for truly they are…superior."

Gasps and whispers filled the sanctuary. Ezra sat down, visibly shaken. And Rebecca just smiled.

For she had him down below…forever.

THE TREE

"Gentlemen, please do not think me a braggart blowing my own horn. I simply speak the truth. I tell you that I have never failed in derring-do. And I dare say that I will never fail. I think it is impossible that I can fail. I believe that I have the spunk and willpower to accomplish any feat that I accept. And so, gentlemen, I continue to welcome proposals from anyone."

Having finished his little speech, Richard Torger lit a cigarette, sipped some wine and waited for someone at the table to comment. He was a middle-aged English adventurer who, during the last few years, had made quite a name for himself—and no small amount of money—by performing dangerous feats proposed to him by wealthy men.

"I say, Torger, would you consider a little dive over Victoria Falls?" asked Wilson. "I'm sure you could do it without breaking a single bone. Your iron covering of ego would certainly protect you from harm."

"Please, gentlemen," spoke Torger, breaking through the snickering that sounded among the men, "let's keep this serious. Will you make sport of a man simply because he happens to always emerge victorious? Is it my fault that I love to beat the devil? Am I to be blamed that it is my chief pleasure to flirt with the reaper—and always cheat him?"

"No, I can't say that you should," Wilson admitted. "You must excuse me, old man, for that comment. It was just too irresistible to pass. Blazes, Torger, we all know well enough about your spunk. And I dare say that every man here admires you and is proud to claim you as a friend."

Wilson was almost correct on this last point. Every man sitting at that table with Torger knew of his daredevil exploits—and the fame and money he had received from performing them. For example, he had once accepted a dare from a very bored millionaire desperate for a wild diversion to swim across the crocodile infested Shibeli River in Somalia. He had accomplished it unscathed, mainly because the crocodiles had preferred the scraps of swine liver he threw them as he swam. Yes, he made it easily; and became seventy thousand pounds sterling richer. Another wealthy man had once dared him to jump three hundred feet into Lake Taganyika from an airplane. Torger did indeed jump; and although, after fishing him out, the witnesses needed to place him in a hospital for serious physical trauma, he survived—his bank account much larger and his ego soaring to new heights. He had once won one hundred thousand dollars from a rich American for remaining twenty-four hours in an eight by ten foot cellar in pitch blackness with twelve king cobras. The serpents had crawled all over him, sometimes flicking his face with their tongues. But he had emerged uninjured, only because he remained absolutely motionless, barely even breathing. And the list of his exploits went on.

Now, Wilson was *almost* correct when he said that every man sitting at that table considered Torger his friend. But there was one person there, another Englishman, who despised him. His name was Linten, James Linten, a loser, more or less, and a noted holder of grudges.

A woman was the reason for this. It was an affair of the heart. Ann was her name, and Linten had loved her desperately. He once thought she had felt the same way towards him, also. But then Torger had entered the scene, and something about him—his looks, his money, his fame or his derring-do itself—had drawn her irresistibly to him. And as for her relationship with Linten, she had simply ended it with a terse little Dear John letter.

And what really grated him about the whole thing was that Torger, who he knew could have had any girl, had taken Ann, *his* girl. And apparently for good, for they had soon married.

And so Linten hated him. He wanted revenge. He now lived only for vengeance. No, he was not considering anything as drastic as murder. The satisfaction received from that act would not be worth the risk of being discovered and hung. And why, after all, should he plan a homicide when there existed a way of obtaining a deeper satisfaction—and without any illegality involved at all? That is, why should he murder Torger when it would be much sweeter to beat him at his own game? What better revenge would it be than to end his successes with dangerous stunts? He knew that it would absolutely crush his enemy to fail at a dare. Besides, he might win a large measure of Torger's money—and also finally prove to Ann that her husband was not such a superman after all.

Linten had spent much time thinking up possible dares to present to Torger, but had rejected them one after the other. The catch was proposing a dare that he was positive Torger, upon accepting it, could not accomplish. That is, he knew he had to trick him into accepting something impossible.

Then he happened to read a particular article in the *National Geographic* about mutual benefits received in certain relationships between insects and plants. And this provided the idea for the perfect dare he could present to Torger. It seemed to have the fail-safe he required. The particular situation he needed, however, might prove difficult to find. Everything had to be perfect. So he hired some men of the Masai tribe to search for it all over Kenya. Several weeks passed, and then a chap named Mokindu reported to him that he had discovered the ideal situation Linten required. It was located, informed Mokindu, in the Great Rift Valley. So, Linten, accompanied by the Masai, traveled to the site, and discovered that it fit his needs exactly. Linten rejoiced; he had the perfect dare with which to trick his nemesis. Everything, though, depended on whether his enemy knew about the nature of a certain species of tree. And Linten was betting on Torger's ignorance.

Upon accosting the daredevil a few days later, Linten propositioned him.

"Well, Torger, so you're still looking for ways to beat the devil, eh? Well, I've found quite a tall tree growing over a cliff that I dare you money to climb."

"A tree, eh? And it grows over a cliff? Well, let's go see this tree, old boy." Torger seemed ready to attempt the feat that very day. Like everyone else, he didn't really care for Linten—and desired to win his money as soon as he could. "I'll climb anything you dare me to climb—for the right price. I'll climb Kilimanjaro itself—in the night and nude—to best you. Hell, I already won your lover; I might as well win your money too!"

* * *

"So what's so fearful and dangerous about this stunt, Linten?" The two men had just arrived at the site of the wager. Torger looked up at Linten's tree and then spoke again. "Are you betting that I'll be too afraid, once up there, to climb out on that limb you pointed out just because it hangs out over this little cliff?" The "little cliff" was a steep drop, about five hundred feet. "Or maybe you're betting that the limb will break and I'll fall to my death, is that it? Well, you're wrong on both counts, old man. First, I'm not the least afraid to crawl out over the drop; and second, I know that that limb will more that support my weight. I know that tamarinds are among the strongest of trees. That limb will not break. Do you want out? It wouldn't be sporting of me not to offer you a chance to back away from this and save your money."

"Come, come, Torger, it won't be that simple," replied Linten—who, although rejoicing over the man's ignorance of the type of tree involved here, did not betray his emotions. "I'm not as big a fool as you might think. It's easy enough, I'm sure, for you to run your mouth down here, but you're not up there yet. You're not looking at the drop from up there, nor can you see from here how really slender that limb is. I say you'll back down before you climb out on it—or fall to your death down the cliff when it breaks with you."

"Very well," spoke Torger, "it's your money to lose. Now, if you would, Wilson, declare the exact nature of this wager, so as to eliminate any possible misunderstanding."

At this, Wilson, who acted as a witness to this dare, now spoke. "As I understand it, gentlemen, the wager concerns this tree. You, Mr. Linten, have offered Mr. Torger an amount of money to climb up to the fifth limb of this tree, then crawl along it to the first fork and, at that point, tie this red handkerchief. Here the bet will be concluded and it will be up to Mr. Torger to descend this tree in any manner he wants. He may use climbing spurs, but nothing else. If he succeeds in tying the handkerchief at the specified point, you, Mr. Linten, must pay him sixty thousand pounds. However, if you, Mr. Torger, for any reason, can not secure the handkerchief at the stated point, you must pay Mr. Linten sixty thousand pounds. I hold both checks on my person, and will surrender both to the winner—or, if the case should be, to Mr. Torger's benefactors in case accident should befall him *after* he succeeds in tying the handkerchief.

"Gentlemen, do you both understand the agreement?"

The two men both declared in the affirmative.

"And do you, Mr. Torger, agree to attempt Mr. Linten's proposition?"

"Of course!" answered the daredevil; "without a doubt!"

"Then begin whenever you are ready."

"Child's play!" Torger declared, as he removed his coat. He was dressed lightly for the task—a thin short sleeved shirt and khaki shorts. And, for some reason, this had caused Linten to smile. Torger knelt down to attach the spurs. When they were secured to his boots, he looked up at the tree again. Then he said, "Really, Linten, I would have expected better of you. I'll get up there, scoot across that limb, tie the cloth and return in no time. And then, old boy, I'll kindly receive your check."

"Then why don't you get about it, old *boy*," cried Linten, "and, for once in your life, stop bragging?"

Without replying to Linten's insulting remark, Torger now arose and approached the tree with all the ease in the world. He glanced up at his first objective, the fifth limb. It was about forty feet up the trunk. It stretched out treacherously over the deep chasm, but he wasn't the least bit intimidated. He grabbed hold of the trunk like a bear, dug in his spurs and started up.

"You know he's going to make it, don't you, Linten," spoke Wilson as they watched him ascend. "You're money's as good as his already."

"Oh, I don't know that at all," Linten replied. "On the contrary, I think you might as well give me his check now."

"I can't believe your confidence," declared Wilson, turning to look at him. "Why, you're just as sure of yourself as he. I just don't understand how you can think that Torger, knowing his reputation as you do, won't accomplish this dare. Even I can see that that limb is perfectly safe; and you should know that he won't hesitate to climb out on it, even if it does hang out over this steep chasm. Just what exactly is your money on?"

At this Linton smiled, looked at the other man and said, "My money is on the tree itself…and a little secret it contains."

"Ow! Blazes, God!… Ahhh!" These sounds came from up above them in the tree. Both men looked up toward the climber, Wilson's face in wonderment, Linten's in glee. They saw Torger, who had stopped just beneath the third limb, slapping himself all about his body.

Linten laughed with satisfaction. Then he called up to his enemy. "It's not a tamarind tree, you fool! Oh, it looks well enough like a tamarind, and that's what I bet on—that as well as your ignorance altogether with this species. Ever hear of a 'mingo' tree, Torger? Well, that's what you're in right now. They are very rare, and, without exception, are always home to an equally rare, but especially nasty, species of ants. Did you ever hear about 'devil ants' Torger? They live in the tree and eat its berries. And as for their part in the arrangement, they protect the mingo from intruders. They kill and eat caterpillars, beetles and other things that might hurt their home. It's called 'mutual benefit.' They'll attack anything that invades the tree—especially some fool sticking spurs into it. They kill you if you stay there. And they don't need much time to do it, either. So come down, you bastard. Come down, you swine, while you still have flesh, and pay me!"

"Linten!" Wilson was aghast. "My God, are you mad!" Then he yelled up to the man in the tree. "Torger, come down! Jump for it if you have to, but come down! Trickery! Your money's safe. The wager is canceled due to trickery!"

At this Linten glared at Wilson with fury and cried, "Hold, sir! How dare you claim this wager is off? I did nothing but make a wager and show him this tree. I told no lies, nor was I obliged to warn him." Then he looked back up in the tree and shouted, "Yes, you'd better come down, Torger. They'll eat you alive if you don't. But the wager's still good, and you must pay. Ha ha ha! How does it feel to finally fail in a daredevil venture?"

But Torger didn't answer. He was still slapping himself violently, but he did not come down. Instead, he suddenly continued climbing *up*!

"Torger!" screamed Linten, "Come down, madman! Face it, you've lost!

"Torger!" Now Wilson yelled. "In God's name come down! You can't make it!"

But their cries fell on deaf ears because Torger was only thinking of preserving—he now knew at the expense of his life—his unbroken string of successful derring-do's. His body was one blaze of fire now, but he kept climbing up, pausing only now and then to brush the enraged biting and stinging insects away from his eyes.

"He's not coming down!" cried Wilson. "He'll need a doctor. Try to call him down, Linten. I'll run to the jeep and radio for help."

And with that, Wilson quickly took off down the trail for the vehicle parked about a mile away.

But Linten didn't call out. Instead, he continued watching in disbelief the figure in the mingo tree. The man was completely covered with ants now, but he kept climbing, and finally made it to the fifth limb. Then he crawled along the limb toward the point where it was stipulated to tie the handkerchief. And as Linten watched him proceed, all he could do was whisper to himself over and over, "The fool...the bloody fool...."

Then, Torger reached the place where the cloth was to be tied. He was perched above hundreds of feet of space, and he was swollen and bleeding from the ants viciously ravaging his body, but he still managed to tie the handkerchief.

And when this was done, Linten beheld the ghastly figure in the tree raise its arm in victory.

"The fool…the bloody fool…." Linten could only still whisper this over and over.

But when he saw the man above him somehow make his way back along to the center part of the mingo and start down, he could hold it in no longer.

"You fool!" he screamed. "You're dead, you bloody fool! You'll never survive this. You'll die long before help arrives. But even if you did survive, you'd never spend any of my money—simply because I don't have any. Ha ha! I was already nearly broke before this affair, and I was obliged to hand over all the remaining cash I had to the Masai for finding this tree for me. I'm bankrupt. I made this bet with you only because it seemed a sure thing. I was certain you'd come down. My only mistake was in not realizing exactly how great a fool you were. You went ahead. You let them eat you alive just to keep your successes intact. But you didn't really win, Torger. Actually *I'm* the winner here. Oh, my reputation as a gentleman of honor will be ruined in Kenya, yes; but your death will be well worth the trouble of moving away and starting over. And mind you, I plan to win Anne back too. So I *am* the winner, Torger! Ha ha, I *am* the winner!"

Torger had reached the second limb by now and found himself directly over the laughing man. He knew he was only minutes from death; already what was left of his flesh was numb to the countless stingers and mandibles. But as he felt himself grow weaker, a desperate idea entered his mind. And so, after brushing the things away from his eyes one final time, and seeing his enemy below through blue halos, he suddenly jumped.

And he landed squarely on his target—on Linten—and knocked him down. Then he embraced him and used every once of his remaining strength to hold on. No matter how hard the surprised Linten tried to break free, he held on. No matter how violently the now alarmed Linten struck out at him, he held on. No matter how desperately the now screaming Linten—he screamed because the vicious things were now crawling all over him, biting and stinging—thrashed and twisted and drug him around, Torger held on.

And that was how Wilson, returning later after radioing for help, found them. They were both dead by then, what was left of Torger the braggart still embraced what was left of Linten the bastard.

But one could not say that this wager had no winners. The *true* winners were the ones rushing to and from the mingo tree—the ones returning to the tree laden with nice little chunks of nourishment.

PUMPANDUMP VERSUS PITCHINDITCH

"The more the dead are respected, the more is God pleased."

—an anonymous idiot

Once upon a time, a time back in the days before undertakers became "funeral directors," there was an average, ordinary, mediocre town known as Gullybully. Today, there still is a Gullybully, but it is no longer *quite* so average, ordinary and mediocre. The records pertaining to its origin, settlement, notable citizens and events and so forth would be just as ho-humish to read about as would the records of any other ordinary town. Ho-humish, that is, until one reads of the great rivalry that once arose between its two funeral homes, for the particulars and the results of this contest explain how Gullybully lost its mediocrity.

Now there was not always active hostility between Mr. Pumpandump's funeral home and the funeral home of Mr. Pitchinditch. I'm referring back to the days when they were not nearly so respectful of the dead. But this must *not* be misunderstood. Far be it from either of these two particular morticians to have ever been wanting in the proper respect of the dearly departed! I was merely alluding to the not too far distant past when the services provided by Gullybully's two funeral homes—as well as the services provided by all funeral homes—were relatively simple. Their duties back then were mainly the following: replace the fluids of the deceased with embalming solution (but only if requested to do so by the deceased's survivors), bathe, clothe and groom the corpse for display, cater a simple ceremony and, finally, provide for the deceased a modest pine coffin and a humble, inexpensive tombstone. And they were reasonable men. They made money from their occupation, of course, but the amount of profit was no more than in fair proportion to the services rendered.

Now, I stated that there was not always animosity between Gullybully's two undertakers, but this, of course, should not imply that they were the best of friends either. Their relationship was, more or less, a matter of peaceful co-existence—as is the relationship usually adopted by most competing establishments. And this stability between Pumpandump and Pitchinditch might have continued to this day—thus probably keeping Gullybully just as average, ordinary and mediocre as it had ever been—had not Mr. Pumpandump decided, one day, to hire an organ player to perform funeral dirges while the kin and friends of the deceased given unto his care visited his parlor to pay their last respects. Now, because an organ and a musician to play it were not available for free, Mr. Pumpandump had no other alternative but to pass the cost of these additions on to his clients. But organ music, he decided, was almost as important to a funeral as the cadaver itself. Why, a funeral just wasn't a funeral without some good old depressing organ dirges, he concluded. And so from then on—although it would make his funerals a bit more costly than those of his competitor—the organ and its player became regular additions to his services.

So he contacted Wrink Inkstink, the editor of the local newspaper, *The Gullybully Times*, and advertised his new feature in this publication; and, surprisingly enough, he soon received all the dead folk business in town. He quickly found himself enjoying a complete monopoly. But, on second thought, it really shouldn't be surprising at all—especially when one considers the profound degree of respect that the good citizens of Gullybully felt for their dead. But even if the music did cost extra, would it not be almost irreverent for *anyone* to deny his dearly departed the honor and respect of having organ dirges played at the deceased's funeral? Horrors and shame! Never think of money when the dead are involved!

Upon realizing that he was no longer receiving any cadavers to fix up and care for, it was only to be expected that Mr. Pitchinditch experienced no small amount of panic. But this was not for any great length of time, for Pitchinditch was much too competent and resourceful a businessman. With the understanding of exactly what had happened to cause this vacancy within his parlor, he not only acquired his own organ and musician, he also exchanged his pine coffins for oak coffins. He then proclaimed in *The Gullybully Times* that he was now featuring, in addition to organ dirges, a selection of "higher quality" receptacles for the dead. His new coffins, he claimed, were not only more beautiful than the plain old pine boxes offered by his competitor; but they would also be *safer* for their precious potential occupants. Oak, he explained (or at least claimed) resisted combustion much better than pine, and as such being the case, the kin and friends of the deceased that were laid to rest in these oak coffins could remain at ease—secure in the knowledge that the remains of their beloved were relatively safe from an accidental fire. Why, even if the funeral home itself burned to the ground, he exclaimed in the paper, his new coffins would, in all probability, protect their precious contents. Now the organ music and the new coffins, he carefully went on to say, were not optional. They were now a regular part of his services, and thus would naturally make his care more costly that the care offered by the other home.

"But my goodness," he exclaimed in the paper, "do the dead deserve less?"

The good people of Gullybully took his words to heart, and all of them with postmortem responsibility started taking their dead exclusively to Pitchinditch. True, it was more expensive, but the Gullybullians (would that we emulate them forever!) were a *respectful* people. They possessed too much reverence for the dead to concern themselves with the price of funerals. But then, how could anyone—whether he lived in Gullybully or elsewhere—sink himself in the fathomless disgrace of thinking of these solemn matters in terms of economics? Horrors and shame! Never think of money when the dead are involved!

Now that both Pumpandump and Pitchinditch knew through experience what wonderful advantages belong to the owner of a monopoly, each undertaker determined to win exclusive and permanent control of Gullybully's dead folk for himself. Pumpandump prepared to wrest control from his rival, and thus the great contest was begun. Contributing to the heat of the conflict, and even making it desperate, was the painful fact that, in a battle of this nature, unless a compromise was agreed upon, bankruptcy and ruin would probably be the fate of the loser.

Soon after Pumpandump had lost the upper hand, the following appeared in *The Gullybully Times*:

> GOOD NEWS! GOOD NEWS! Pumpandump Funeral Home is proud to announce the arrival of a shipment of metal—repeat—METAL caskets. While our competitors can only claim that their oak containers may only probably—repeat—PROBABLY safeguard their occupants from fire, we issue a guarantee with every casket we provide that insures protection from fire 100%! Unlike oak, metal is absolutely fireproof! Thus we at Pumpandump can promise you that in one of our metal caskets, your dearly departed mother, or whoever died that you are responsible for, would never suffer the tragedy of turning to ash before her due and proper time.
>
> BUT WAIT! THAT'S NOT ALL! Our new caskets are not only completely fireproof, but are also absolutely invulnerable to termites, ants, worms and all manner of crawling things. Imagine how happy your mother's soul would be if it knew its physical remains were safe from the ravages of these vile pests. Well, now she can *really* rest in peace—as long as she rests in one of our new, beautiful and safe metal caskets. Can our competitors make such a claim? Remember our motto: "*First* to Pumpandump, *then* to heaven."
>
> Notice: Because our higher, more profound degree of consideration and respect for the deceased does not allow us to keep in stock any receptacles inferior to our new metal caskets, we have no choice but to raise our prices to cover the added expense. But remember: We are discussing

> the consideration that is only due and proper to those of us who have passed on. At Pumpandump we RESPECT the dead! But to anyone who would be insensitive enough, irreverent enough and, yes, shameful enough to actually concern himself over the extra cost of our more virtuous methods of respecting the deceased, we would suggest that he give his deceased unto our cheaper competitors. Yes, give your dear mother to the other home if you are not one to be governed by morals. Go ahead, give her to *them* if you are not concerned about the possibility of her precious remains being burned to ash! Give her to *them*! The worms will thank you.

How inconsistent is the way the wind blows! As far as Pitchinditch was concerned, after this advertisement, people had stopped dying.

But he was not distressed for any undue length of time, for was it not mentioned earlier that Pitchinditch was a competent and resourceful businessman in the undertaking profession? He realized that if he were to recapture the monopoly, the replacement of his oak coffins for metal caskets would not be enough. No, that would merely stabilize the situation, leaving things as they were before the contest had begun. Pitchinditch wanted *all* of Gullybully's dead people for himself, and to accomplish this, he understood that he must, in addition to furnishing his own line of metal caskets, introduce another new feature.

Now Pitchinditch had many friends living in Gullybully, and among them was a very prominent physician, a certain Dr. Rob A. Sickfellow. And it was through this doctor's tip off that Mr. Pitchinditch happened to learn of a certain Gullybullyian lately incapacitated by a serious condition of the blood vessels. (I am sure that the reader is familiar with this illness. It is characterized by the damming up of the blood flowing back to the heart due to the compressed and interfering relationship of the blood vessels to one another. You know... "very-close-veins"?) Pitchinditch was very interested in this particular case. After all, this sick person might kick the bucket at any time, and Pitchinditch wanted to beat Pumpandump to the scene and be the first to discuss with the dying man's relatives the matter of which funeral home they would decide on.

With great anticipation did Pitchinditch wait for the inevitable. Why, there wasn't a day that passed that did not witness a trip by Mr. Pitchinditch to the local medical institution, Mercy for Much Money Hospital, to visit the dying man and his family. (Why, I wonder, am I suddenly reminded of one of those large disgusting birds that circle in the sky above a carcass?) But please do not misinterpret the undertaker's motives here. His visits were based solely on his genuine concern for this poor man. Every day he expressed his well wishes both to the afflicted person and his family. And when the man finally relinquished the ghost, the undertaker was the very first to succumb to his emotions. (Pitchinditch was superb! He was anything but grieved, but he would have fooled anyone with his weeping and gnashing of teeth.) He soon, however, managed to regain his composure (it was rather quickly, I would think, for one who had been so hysterical with grief just a minute before), and it was then that the solemn, but necessary subject of the funeral arrangements "just happened to enter his mind." Upon introducing this somber subject into the discourse, he explained a new feature he had lately included in his services. Oh, he had already discarded his oak coffins for metal ones, but that wasn't what he was talking about. He was talking about something different, something new and something only his parlor now offered. It seemed that while his competitor, Pumpandump, was apparently satisfied with the old, even dogmatic, ideals concerning the proper respect for the dead, *he,* Pitchinditch, had been thinking of better ways to honor the dearly departed. It was simple: *he,* Pitchinditch, professed more *respect* for the dead than did his "stagnant" competitor. And therefore the grieving family would do much worse in surrendering the corpse to anyone but himself.

Pitchinditch had been careful and subtle in discussing these matters, and when he was certain that he had prevailed over the consciences of those listening to him—certain, that is, that they would feel too guilty to do anything other than what Pitchinditch suggested—he explained to them his new feature. And it is almost needless to state, I suppose, that the bereaved family ended up entrusting the body to the more "respectful" of Gullybully's two funeral homes. And because this transaction proved the feasibility of the innovation (or, more properly, how idiotic and gullible people can be), Pitchinditch communicated to the public the following day in *The Gullybully Times*:

> ATTENTION! ATTENTION! We at Pitchinditch Funeral Home have splendid news for the families and friends of those who are soon to depart this life. But first, may we ask you a question: Do you believe that your mother could *really* rest in peace if she were fated to decompose right along with something that caused her misery, embarrassment or even death? Because we at Pitchinditch have examined this tragic question and concluded that something must be done to remedy this evil, we are very proud and happy to announce our new policy, R.I.P.O.F.F. What is R.I.P.O.F.F., you ask? Well, technically it stands for Removal of Injurious Parts out Finally and Forever, but we will explain it in more simple terms.
>
> Suppose someone very close to you—let us use your mother as an example—happened to succumb to the terrible disease, very-close-veins. Now, even though she suffered and died because of these veins, does that mean that she should have to tolerate their hateful company in her grave? Because we at Pitchinditch feel that it would be inconsiderate and certainly disrespectful to allow this tragedy—there now being a remedy

available—to continue (and you simply *must* agree with us—that is if you *really* love and respect your mother), we have lately made it a part of our policy to remove those hateful very-close-veins from your mother's remains before she is laid to rest! Yes, we would remove them from her, leaving her free of their despicable presence in her body once and for all.

But we have given you only one example. We will remove any thing(s) from your deceased he/she might have despised whether it caused the death or not. For instance, your recently deceased father need not share our recently arrived fire and insect proof metal caskets with that enormous, humped nose he was always ashamed of. Your sister need not be buried with those big bozo ears that always stuck out on her head. We will take care of those big ugly feet. We'll trim the fat.

Notice: Because our respect for dead people is too sincere and profound to allow us to stock any receptacles for corpses other than the new metal and, we must add, more expensive caskets, we have no alternative but to raise our prices. Also, we practice R.I.P.O.F.F. at a standard fee of $500. Of course this is an optional feature; we *CANNOT* perform it unless it is requested by our clients. But then again we *CANNOT* believe that any person, whether healthy or dying, is perfectly satisfied with his/her body. And that is why we encourage you to find out right now, if you don't already know, what that rapidly expiring relative you are responsible for hates about him/herself.

It was not a very long time after this ad appeared in the paper that Pitchinditch again found himself enjoying complete control of Gullybully's dead people. And as for his rival, Pumpandump? Well, obviously, with his parlors vacant, he suffered no small amount of alarm. But he was also very angry. Sooo! Pitchinditch was going to play it *that* way, eh? Well, *he*, Pumpandump, could play this game even rougher! Yeah, he would show him. He would show Pitchinditch how to *really* pull the shroud—a woolen shroud, that is, over their eyes.

Now as much as he hated to admit it to himself, Pumpandump admired his competitor's new policy of R.I.P.O.F.F., and he wished this great idea had been his own. Of course, he was going to adopt the same feature anyway; for this was necessary to stabilize the situation. But if he were to regain the monopoly—and this he certainly intended to do—he understood that he must introduce yet another new feature to capture all the mortuary business. After considerable deliberation, he decided to simply enlarge upon R.I.P.O.F.F. And to discover exactly what he did, let us again turn to *The Gullybully Times* and read his advertisement:

> GOOD NEWS! GOOD NEWS! Pumpandump Funeral Home—always changing and improving with the times in order to provide the best of consideration and respect for the dearly departed people of Gullybully—has lately adopted the policy of ridding the dead of despicable body parts, which, though known under different names, we have entitled Avenge-A-Body. With Avenge-A-Body, we not only remove from your dead mother those misery and/or death causing parts, *but also enable you to AVENGE your mother on those very same loathsome organs!*!
>
> But the best thing about it is that this opportunity is absolutely free as our gift to you! It works like this: You pay the cost, $600, of our skilled surgeons to remove what your mother hated; *then we hand back over to you what was removed for no additional charge*! Then, with fists, feet, or even spit, you can demonstrate to your dear mother's

> ghost how much *you* hate whatever part(s) *she* hated! Show the spirits of any of your dearly departed that you mean business! Pound your daddy's ugly buck teeth of two bits! Smush that huge Adam's apple that protruded from Uncle Joe's throat so repulsively with a pair of pliers! Put a match to that sprawling mass of cancerous hair that finished off Aunt Ethel! Squish those disgusting fishy goggle eyes of Cousin Edna with a rolling pin!

(Now, I hate to imply anything, but was it just a *coincidence* that, soon after this, the local meat market also placed an ad in the paper soliciting the services of two new butchers?)

Do I really need to state that after the good people of Gullybully read this in the paper that the wind blew the other way? But, then again, do I need to add that Mr. Pitchinditch gave up and went kite flying? As it turned out, he simply countered Pumpandump's move by ordering a wardrobe of very elegant and quite expensive burial apparel.

"HALLELUJAH!" he exclaimed in the paper. "PRAISE THE LORD!" And then, following these tried-and-true words of getting attention from people, he fed the Gullybullians his pitch. "Yes, at Pitchinditch Funeral Home we're singing hallelujah and praising the Lord. And that is because we're getting ready, or rather, getting the dead ready, for that oncoming day of days, Resurrection and Judgment Day! Who knows," asked Pitchinditch, "it could be just around the corner! And that is why we've decided it is high time to clad the bodies given to us in apparel only proper for that magnificent occasion. You wouldn't want your mother to rise up from the grave to meet the Lord clothed in her plain old Sunday dress, would you? Would you desire your resurrected father to behold the glory of God dressed in a drab old monkey suit? Of course not! That is why we at Pitchinditch have supplied our funeral home with nothing but the best in formal clothing—

everything from Parisian evening gowns to tuxedos straight from London.

"Pick up a Good Book," added Pitchinditch, "and read for yourself what it says about this: 'If the Day of Judgment had only been ascertained to be a dress day, everyone there would have been eternally correct.'" (Now, although the preceding sentence was *not* from the Bible, Pitchinditch had not really printed an outright lie. It was from Charles Dickens' *A Tale of Two Cities*, and, as most people would agree, that piece of literature is a pretty "good book.")

Finally, after adding that he, too, would hand over, for no charge, the parts and pieces left over from R.I.P.O.F.F. for purposes of revenge, he concluded the ad by introducing the people to his new motto: "Dig up your mother. And if she was buried by Pitchinditch, you'd find her smiling."

Now notwithstanding the fact that a Pitchinditch funeral, with its fancy burial wear, now cost more money that a Pumpandump funeral, the good people of Gullybully started giving their dead exclusively unto the care of the former. Yes, it was more costly, but the people of Gullybully possessed *consciences.* They professed too much respect and consideration for their dead to even consider denying the deceased the proper apparel for Resurrection and Judgment Day. (But would it not be unspeakably shameful for *anyone* to deny his departed the opportunity to make a good impression with his clothing on the Lord when He finally comes? Is it not just a matter of proper, divine vogue?

But the contest was by no means concluded. Pumpandump was not about to concede anything to his competitor—not as long as there was such conscientious respect for the deceased in this town. (Why, these poor fools were conscientious enough to feel guilty about refusing dead people *anything*—even if it did mean their ending up in the poor house.) And so, with this in mind, Pumpandump first ordered his own wardrobe of formal wear, then he introduced tombstones embellished with, at least what he claimed, was ivory.

"Come in and browse through *our* line of formal burial wear," he invited them via the paper. "And while you're here, look over our new selection of monuments adorned with genuine INDIAN ELEPHANT IVORY! Give your dead mother some real class! Give her some real respect!"

And the wind, thanks to Pumpandump's gaudy-looking, but very expensive tombstones, changed yet again.

As time passed, and as the great struggle continued to seesaw back and forth, the funerals in Gullybully became so expensive that its citizens eventually realized that it had become practical, even necessary, for all to equally share the cost of each funeral no matter who was actually responsible. Thus each individual was insured financial help when one of his own beloved passed on.

After all, golden caskets do not come cheap.

Meanwhile, Pumpandump and Pitchinditch were becoming quite the affluent businessmen. In fact, by the time the people had joined together to share the expenses of each funeral bill, they were the wealthiest men in the whole town. And it was around this time when the two morticians decided that the term "undertaker" was too crude and insensitive a title for their occupation. And so from then on, then, Pumpandump and Pitchinditch—and, at least in America, all other morticians as well—became "funeral directors." Actually, the term "undertaker," aside from being too "crude" and "insensitive" a word, is also too precise and truthful. After all "undertaking," or "taking under," is exactly what funeral directors do. They "take" all kinds of people "under"—especially the living ones.

The great rivalry continued on through the years; and as time passed, the later you died in Gullybully, the better off you were, because the respect and considerations for the dead kept growing and growing.

But finally the day arrived when the contest was suddenly ended. It happened as a result of the decision of the two parties involved to merge their two clip joints into one organization: P.P. Funerals Inc. (Due to the unresolved problem of whose name should precede the other, Pumpandump and Pitchinditch decided to simply, but officially, use their initials, the two *P's,* instead of their full last names. Thus, whether the title of their company was *Pumpandump,* Pitchinditch Funerals Inc. or *Pitchinditch,* Pumpandump Funerals Inc. was never determined. It was simply P.P.…on everyone in Gullybully.)

And now let us examine the details of the great merger, the proclamation of which made the headlines in, of course, *The Gullybully Times*:

> "IT IS OVER! IT IS OVER! PUMPANDUMP AND PITCHINDITCH ARE ONE! Pumpandump Funeral Home and Pitchinditch Funeral Home are happy to announce that their long lasting struggle concerning the best and most proper methods of bestowing respect for the deceased of Gullybully is now officially concluded with a merger. Pumpandump Funeral Home and Pitchinditch Funeral Home are now officially P.P. Funerals Inc. The following is the official statement:
>
> "'Let it be known that we, the proprietors of Gullybully's two funeral institutions, having concluded that it is only in the best interest of the good citizens of Gullybully, have united our two parlors together into one establishment. We believe that in combining our two parlors—that is, in working together instead of at odds—we can provide the people of Gullybully with opportunities to pay their dearly dead beloved nothing less than the MOST supreme respect!'
>
> "So as of today, your dead mother can enjoy all the respect she truly deserves. She'll at last be happy; she'll at last be content; for she'll be in the care of P.P. Funerals Inc.!"

Thus, according to the paper's headlines (and if the headlines seemed more like an advertisement for their parlor, it was because, by this time, Pumpandump and Pitchinditch *owned The Gullybully Times*—not to mention everything else in town, including the hospital, the bank, and city hall), the two funeral directors had merged solely because it was "only in the best interest of the good citizens of Gullybully." (Actually what had happened was that these two rogues had realized that if they put their heads together in a mutual understanding, they could take these ridiculous fools for every cent they had!) And it wasn't a very long time following the great merger that Mr. Pumpandump and Mr. Pitchinditch decided that it was "only in the best interest in the good citizens of Gullybully" that P.P. Funerals Inc. offer the people the new feature—not optional, by the way—of modern mummification of the dead. And after the so-called scientists, chemists and Egyptologists contracted by P.P. had claimed to develop a contemporary technique based on the methods used by the ancients from the land of the Nile, the two crooks communicated through their paper the glorious news to the people. And I suppose it is needless to state that the idiots of Gullybully, every single one of them, went for it hook, line and sinker.

But before I tell you what eventually happened to Gullybully, I feel I must first present this very tragic question: What about all of the people who lived in the times before morticians decided to present mourners the chance to respect their dead in such proper, sincere and modern manners? What about the people who were buried in simple, cheap pine boxes and whose graves were marked by modest, inexpensive stone markers? *God, stay Thy rage!*—what about those unfortunate people, a long time ago, whose remains were simply placed on piles of wood and consumed with fire! The fate of all those poor souls was very sad, indeed; but it is best that we do not grieve over them unduly. After all, if we consider this for too long a time, we might someday realize what a real difference it makes. That is, we might come to understand what buried in a nice and fancy, expensive casket actually means to a cold, unthinking corpse!

But again, it is advised that we—at least those of us who are proud to be members of the more "civilized" nations of this earth—do not ponder over this. All we can do is make certain that the dead of today receive the higher degree of respect that was not available to the dead of the past. And it is to our credit that most of us are not guilty of the insensitivity, irreverence and, most of all, DISRESPECT that plainly motivates, and in which is clearly revealed, any desire or insistence for simpler, less expensive funerals for our loved ones. *Horrors and shame! Never think of money when the dead are involved!*

Pumpandump and Pitchinditch! Hail to them for inspiring us all to give more comfort, consideration and respect to those that need and deserve it the most: corpses.

Yes, we owe them a lot for what they have accomplished, especially Gullybully. That's why the town doesn't have any money anymore. (And that, by the way, is also why Pumpandump and Pitchinditch departed Gullybully forever. They sailed over the sea to England, where they each purchased, and retired within, his own huge, lavish castle.) But Gullybully still exists, even so. And unless the planet ends within the foreseeable future, it shall continue to exist for unknown eons to come.

Or at least the architecture shall. The Gullybullians, however, will not be so fortunate. They are doomed for complete extinction—to pass forever away like those first classical people who once dwelt along the River Nile and worshiped their pharaohs as gods. But this is only the way the citizens themselves prefer it. The Gullybullians, understand, have became a very strange, scary people. They have become absolutely preoccupied, yes, even enamored, with death. It has become like a deity to them. And because they hold this event in such sacred awe, it has become taboo for them to propagate. They detest life. It is their enemy. They want nothing good or grand to do with life anymore, and this includes the sun, itself. And thanks to P.P. Funerals Inc., they no longer have to tolerate that body's light and warmth. They creep about their town in perpetual night, never venturing outside the town, nor even desiring to. In fact, it is now quite impossible to either enter or leave Gullybully. For P.P. Funeral

Inc.'s final innovation—which, according to the two funeral directors, was THE ultimate and most sincere act of respecting the dead of Gullybully for all time—entombed the entire town within a massive, geometrical structure.

Egypt may still boast of her pyramids, or at least in their antiquity. But the Great Pyramid of Cheops is no longer the greatest.

DORIAN NECROMANCED

"The dead make suspect companions, and even worse lovers."

—Nordica Primrose

Sylvia Mates was one of those young women who people tend to shun. She had always been a loner, more or less. Back during her school days, it was said she had a case of the "cooties," those mysterious little creeping things that supposedly infest certain undesirables. And although most people know that there are actually no such organisms, Sylvia repelled her classmates anyway. They had just considered her gross. Back in school, she had suffered from pimples. No matter how diligently she attended to her face, trying all sorts of ointments, creams or salves, there always seemed to be at least one on her face, usually oozing with infection. She was always pressing on them, but just making them worse with the irritation. And to add to her woes, she had had a severe case of dandruff. No matter how often she shampooed, she could not seem to rid her scalp of the flakes. And it itched terribly. Sometimes so terribly that she forgot herself, and applied fingernails to scalp vigorously in public. One particular day—and she still winced when she remembered—her scalp itched so fiercely, it was unendurable. So, hardly conscious of her surroundings, she literally attacked her head with her fingernails, raking her scalp with them. How long she scratched, she did not remember. But when she overheard some guy whisper to the teacher, "Get her out of here," she immediately stopped and suffered extreme embarrassment. She had wished that the floor would open up and swallow her.

Yes, she had had a very rough time in school. But although those days were long gone, things really had not improved much for her. Now, as a woman in her thirties, the pimples and dandruff were gone, but she still had no social life to speak of. People still seemed to keep their distance from her—as if the cooties were still there—thus she had no friends. And Sylvia, who desperately needed friends—who just wanted to fit in somewhere—often cried herself to sleep.

It was a sad thing, indeed. For if she had not suffered from, call it, "negative body vibes" or a "bad aura," she might have actually possessed a boyfriend. She was not half bad looking; and she was a very sweet person. But although she desired a soul mate more than anything, all men shied away from her. It was just like high school. They ignored her, even avoided her. And so she was reduced to sneaking glances at them, and fantasizing. She hung out in places where men were sure to be, like the post office or library. Those were excellent locales to steal looks. But it was awful when they caught her looking at them, and they would return a vicious *What the fuck are you looking at, creep?* glare. This always crushed her. Finally she had to give this pathetic practice up. She decided it was simply not worth the risk of being discovered gazing at them.

Poor Sylvia. She was a lovesick idiot who craved love, but never received love. And so she became an avid moviegoer. The films became her only source of comfort. She loved to watch the handsome, glamorous actors perform on celluloid. At least in the theaters, she could gaze at the pretty boys on the big screen without fear of being caught. And later on at home, at least she could daydream about romantic encounters with them.

Yes, she loved several of the stars, but her favorite one by far, the one she loved most of all, was an English actor known simply as Dorian—who had adopted the name from the Oscar Wilde character in the famous story *The Picture of Dorian Grey*. He represented everything she cherished in a man. She adored him, worshiped him. She *loved* him—and so did the camera. Simply put, he had the perfect face. The few and small lines were all in the right places, and his complexion was flawless. His piercing gray eyes were irresistible, and they were well complemented by the other pleasing aspects of his face. The shape of his head was noble, even kingly, and it was set off splendidly by thick locks of curly raven black hair hanging freely about the neck. As for his build, it could have been a model for a statue of Achilles. And he liked tight pants—tight pants with cod pieces. For he liked to emphasize himself.

As it was implied, Sylvia was crazy about him. She had seen every movie he had starred in countless times and had a mountain of the magazines that featured him. No girl worshiped him like she did—no girl fantasized about him as much. She had a veritable mental treasure chest of daydreams about the two of them.

One of the fantasies involved herself pretending that she was a beautiful princess in peril. She was chained to a rock by a wicked wizard who intended to feed her to his dragon. All seemed lost, but then her prince, Dorian, in shining armor would gallop up on his steed, slay the dragon, kill the wizard and free her. Then they would ride away to lose each other in themselves. A clichéd daydream, yes, but still enjoyed by Sylvia—as it is probably still enjoyed by females worldwide.

Or, more originally, she would picture herself dressed in a long flowing white gown walking upon the White Cliffs of Dover, lonely for her lover. Then he would suddenly appear, again riding a magnificent horse, and clothed in a black coat and cape. He would lift her up behind him on the mount. Then the steed would spout great white wings and spring forth into the ether. They would fly far up into paradise, where fairytale lords and ladies dwelt in fairytale castles, and reside in each other's arms forever.

When Dorian suddenly died of an overdose of heroin, one might well have expected Sylvia, considering how she idolized this person, to have seriously considered suicide. But this was not the case. On the contrary, she was glad at this event. She found herself actually rejoicing over his death. This might have seemed unbelievable at first, but, upon understanding just how Sylvia's mind worked, it would not appear to be so strange. Sylvia, understand, was a devout believer in the afterlife. An avid devotee of the supernatural, she was led to believe that she could communicate with Dorian's now free-floating spirit. Now that he was released from the prison of his body, she reasoned that he was privy to all knowledge—including the existence of herself. Surely, or so she reasoned, he now knew of the love she felt for him. And because she considered it the most sincere, the most devout love of all, surely he would feel the same. And, once psychic communication was established between them, why, anything was possible. He could send her sweet dreams. He could arrange to present her with actual physical gifts. And, the most glorious thing of all: he might just come to her, manifested in a new, immortal body.

And so Sylvia sent out "mental mail" to Dorian. She asked for dreams, for keepsakes, for visits. She prayed to him to see his very soul.

But Dorian did not seem to be listening to her. Or, if he was listening, he apparently did not choose to respond. For months Sylvia prayed. She tortured her mind with entreaty and prayer. She clasped her hands tightly; she wore her knees out. In short, she prayed her brains out. But Dorian did not answer. Instead, she only got slapped in the face with nightmares about malignant phantoms coming to her bedside in the darkness.

And so, she decided to seek help elsewhere. She needed some learned one to advise her. And she knew just who to contact. It was her aunt, Nordica Primrose.

Now, everyone was afraid of old Nordica—Sylvia included. But, nevertheless, people often sought out her assistance with their problems. For Nordica had a way with helping people, if they had the money, that is, by supernatural means. Yes, the old crone was supposed to be quite the enlightened one. She knew about magic—both white and black. She was rumored to be *the* quintessential witch, so Sylvia gathered her courage and went to see her.

The old house Aunt Nordica inhabited seemed to fit right in with the old woman's reputation. It looked just about as haunted as a house could be. Indeed, as she was ushered in the door by her aunt, Sylvia half expected to hear moans up in the attic and chains rattling down in the basement. And as for the owner, it was easy to see how the rumors sprang up around her. Attired in a long black dress that drug the floor, Aunt Nordica looked like something right out of Halloween. She even had a black cat, which hissed and spat at Sylvia.

Aunt Nordica bade her niece to sit down in the kitchen at a massive chestnut table. Then she asked the young woman the reason for her visit.

And Sylvia opened up her heart to the old hag. She went right into her whole unhappy life—how she had never enjoyed true friendship and no social life at all. She related how desperately she had always wanted a boyfriend, but always in vain. Then she mentioned her obsession with Dorian, the movie star. She told how he died and how she had tried, to no avail, to contact his spirit. She related how she expected him to appear to her—in an immortal, uncorrupted body. Then she broke down and wept bitterly. All of the pain, all of the torment, all of the loneliness she had suffered flowed out with the tears. She begged her aunt to help her.

Then Aunt Nordica spoke: "Child, cease your crying. Things are seldom as bad as they seem. I can easily help you obtain a lover—if you really do desire such an unimportant, superficial thing."

Sylvia quickly perked up. "Can you get me Dorian? He's the only one I want."

"Child, you possess no knowledge of what you ask. The dead make suspect companions, and even worse lovers."

"I don't care. Please, Aunt Nordica, if you can, get me my Dorian."

"But he would not be whole."

"Yes, he would. He would make himself whole for me!"

Aunt Nordica rubbed her lips with her hand, lost in contemplation. Then she ventured, "Well, let me check the Akashic Records, then. I need to know what kind of fellow this Dorian was. Wait now, for a few minutes."

The woman then left the room, returning a few moments later with a curious bit of stone covered with strange script. Then she sat down, took a very deep breath and tilted her head way back. She began murmuring in some unknown tongue and rocking from side to side. Finally, with her whole body shaking violently, she released a piercing scream. She next collapsed to the floor in a heap, breathing heavily. For several moments she lay there as if in a seizure. But finally recovering, she arose, sat down in the chair and again spoke.

"Sylvia, my dear one, blood of my blood, I implore you to forget this fellow. He was no good, a very blight on mankind. He committed many dark deeds. He was cruel; he was a liar. His ego knew no bounds. He was a womanizer. He was a vindictive, selfish, self-centered creature. If I summoned him forth for you, he would in all probability return as a ghoul. You should not desire that I call him forth from the grave for you."

"But I *do* want you to call him from the dead," protested Sylvia. "I don't care what he did in his life. He would not hurt me; he would sense that I love him too much. And he would be whole. For me, he *would* be whole. Aunt Nordica, you're the only person in the world who ever cared a little for me. If you refuse to do this, you will break my heart!"

"Child, you prick me to the soul. How can I, then, refuse you? You've given me no choice but to fulfill your request. But, mind you, I still believe it is wrong. I believe only evil can come of this; but I shall help you. I shall get you Dorian. I shall necromance him for you. And, now, remain here; I must fetch the necessary articles for the act."

So the old woman, then, prepared to employ her arts for the second time that day. When she was ready, she proceeded, with white chalk, to draw a very large pentagram on the wooden floor. Within this design, she drew a circle. Next, she placed black candles at each point of the pentagram and lit them. Then she stepped inside the circle and began the incantation.

She started chanting, very softly, words which Sylvia believed were Latin. For a full half hour the old woman chanted, meanwhile slowing turning counterclockwise within the circle. She was very careful not to step outside of it. When she had finished her reciting, she suddenly produced a large vial, it seemed, out of nowhere and threw from it a bright, glowing red liquid. This sparkling substance defied the law of gravity by remaining suspended in the air—

undulating and sizzling. Then, back to English, she shouted out additional words:

"O mighty, O dreadful, O terrible Bell, Xth-clp-nodth! Hearken, now, unto thy servant. I bid thee make thyself manifest before me!"

And before her startled eyes, Sylvia witnessed the thing her aunt had summoned materialize out of the liquid in the air before the old woman. It was an ugly, black, evil looking thing, with unknown hieroglyphic scrip etched all over it.

Then the crone grasped the rope tied to the bell-thing and shouted out: *"Dorian, Sylvia...Dorian, Sylvia...Ego sum te pato ed videre queo!"* And she rang the monstrosity. Sylvia put her hands to her ears; the peals were shattering, cacophonic and cacodemonic. The reverberations seemed to linger and linger, fading very slowly. And as they faded, so too did the bell. Finally all sight and sound of the blasphemous thing faded completely. It being now safe to venture out of the circle, Nordica extinguished the candles and stepped out.

For a long while neither of the two spoke. Sylvia was caught up in awe and contemplation of the startling events that had recently transpired. As for Aunt Nortica, she was too exhausted to speak. But finally Sylvia ventured a question.

"Is it over, Aunt Nortica?"

"Aye," replied her aunt, "I'm all done." She was breathing rapidly, still drained from the ordeal.

"But where is he?" inquired the niece. "When will Dorian come to me? I thought he would appear right after the spell was finished."

"He shall indeed come to you," answered the old woman; "but it will take time. Much time. Remember, he has a ways to travel. But, patience... In time, he *shall* come to you."

Then Aunt Nordica handed Sylvia another vial. It contained another shinny looking, bright fluid. But this time the substance was green.

Then the old woman spoke again. "Now, one final word: take this vial with you and keep it on your person. For if you find him a danger to you when he comes, throw the vial at his feet and say, *'Reditus, creatura, statim ad regum mortuorum.'* I hope you shall not need to use it, but I fear that you shall. Therefore, I advise you to remember these words well. And now, my child, I ask you to depart. Necromancy is an exhausting business. I must lie down."

Sylvia, respectful of her aunt's request, obeyed. And as she drove home, she hummed and sang to herself. For she was happy, happy with the knowledge that her true love would one day finally come to her.

And meanwhile, far away across the Atlantic, something stirred in an English grave.

Who's Dorian? Lately, Sylvia chuckled to herself as this question sometimes popped in her mind. For now, events had changed. Yes, they had changed, as things always do, either for the better or for the worse. And for Sylvia, events had definitely changed for the better. Three months had passed by, and Dorian had failed to appear; but now she didn't care a bit. For Sylvia had finally found someone to love. And this time, her feelings were returned. This was no pathetic, love-you-from-a-distance, imaginary affair. No, there was nothing imaginary about David. He had hands that actually caressed her. And a real body that she could, for the first time in her life, hold tightly. He had a real face that she could touch and kiss. David was no screwed up, arrogant actor. He was real; he was down to earth. And he loved her.

They had met in a laundromat. Sylvia had accidentally dropped her load of clothes on the floor. As she bent down to pick them up—and it was just like slapstick—she had bumped heads with this boy, David, who had also bent down to pick up her clothes. David apparently did not think Sylvia was repellent. He evidently did not think she was gross, or weird, or anything of the kind. Soon they were in full, lively conversation. Never before had a guy acted so nice to her. He was as sweet as cotton candy. And before it was all over, he had even asked her out. At first, Sylvia was embarrassed over how quickly she had acquiesced; but later on, following their date—a nice little picnic in the park—she wasn't worried about it. In fact, later on, while they hugged and kissed and lost their innocence in her apartment, she wasn't worried about anything.

As time passed, their relationship grew stronger and stronger. They had not yet discussed marriage; but to cement their love, they gave each other tokens of their affection for one another. These keepsakes, they wore with pride. David had given Silvia his old St. Christopher medal, with which she now adorned her neck. In return, she had given him her deceased father's gold banded, ruby garnished Masonic ring that she cherished. It was even embellished with a jeweled *D* on the stone—because her father's name had been David also. It fit him perfectly. Yes, to many, this would all seem quite cornball, even immature. It was like things kids did in high school, but they didn't care. They were lost in love.

And as for Dorian? He was ancient history with her. To her he was now just an asshole who had succumbed to money and fame and drugs. Nor was she worried about his coming to claim her. After all, it had been two months since he had supposedly been summoned. No, he wasn't coming. But, just in case, she kept the vial with the green fluid in her purse anyway.

And then came a certain stormy spring night. Never, thought Sylvia, had a storm ever been so violent. Soon, lightening had knocked out the power all over her neighborhood. It was kind of scary, for it seemed especially dark this night; and the thunder and lightning were downright menacing. But David was supposed to come over—in fact, he was already overdue—and she would be safe in his arms. As she was walking around and groping in the darkness for the candles, she suddenly heard a knocking, a slow knocking at her door. She heard three knocks…slow but hard.

"Come in, David," she called.

But David did not enter. Instead, three more knocks were sounded…slow…hard.

Sylvia did not repeat her vocal invitation. Thinking that the door was locked, she, blinded with the night, managed to walk to it. Then she opened it.

It was very dark outside. She could barely discern the figure standing outside the door. It was motionless. It was silent.

"David?" Sylvia almost whispered the name.

The figure remained quiet and motionless. It simply stood there, barely perceptible in the wet darkness. Then Sylvia gagged. A gust of wind suddenly blew a horrible stench her way. Then lightening lit up the sky. It only illuminated the night for a couple of seconds. But those two seconds of light were enough for Sylvia to see the nature of her visitor. And she screamed.

For *he* had finally come to her. Come to claim his own. It had taken three months to cross the Atlantic, but he had, at long last, definitely arrived. The smell was suffocating. He was rotten. And he was bloated with sea water. He was naked. And although some of it had rotted away, there was still enough left of his manhood to present an erection.

Sylvia screamed again. She recoiled from the figure and stumbled back through the darkness into the living room. In complete terror and panic, she found the couch and hid behind it. But he knew exactly where she was. She could hear him shuffling and stumbling toward her hiding place. Then she felt something cold and mushy grasp her arm. Again she screamed, and tried to free herself from the grip. She beat against him with her free hand, but it was no use. Then she felt something else. He rubbed it against her leg. And she was filled with even more terror and revulsion.

Then she somehow remembered the vial. It was supposed to be in her purse, which she prayed was on the nearby coffee table. As the thing clutched and tore at her clothes, she struggled to reach the table. Adrenalin gave her the strength to drag the stinking, decayed thing along with her to the table. Reaching there, she frantically groped along the top of the table for the purse. An eternity in hell passed before she finally felt and grabbed the article. She reached in and, following a few more moments of desperate groping, felt the vial. She quickly drew it out and immediately flung it to the floor at his feet. As the container broke, the green stuff, whatever it was, sizzled on the floor. Then she recited the words old Aunt Nordica had taught her:

"Reditus creatura, statim ad regmum mortuorum!"

And instantly a whirlwind of green fire rose up around the thing, completely engulfing it. Howling with rage, the thing slowly dissolved away with the fire. Then, low, mocking laughter was heard. It echoed and echoed, finally dying out along with the fire.

Sylvia, exhausted, sank down on the couch, sobbing hysterically. She sat there in the darkness, trying to register in a sane way the horrible event that had just transpired.

Then the power suddenly returned, lighting up the room...and she screamed yet again. For she saw something lying on the floor near the door. It was something *he* had brought along with him. It was an arm—an arm that revealed evidence of being gnawed on. *He* must have known. *He* must have been jealous. For there was something Sylvia recognized on one of the fingers. It was a gold-banded, ruby-garnished Masonic ring with a jeweled *D* embellished on the stone.

OUT OF THE PLEIADES

"Aye, the stars do twinkle, but not all, necessarily, with benevolence."

—A certain visionary enamored with the night sky.

I
The Summoning

It might have had something to do with the whole cosmic arrangement in that certain year, or it might have had something to do with destiny—whatever that word actually implies. Or it might have had something to do with the will of God, Himself. Perhaps He perceived the time nearing and declined to interfere. Or maybe he could not interfere; for God is, perhaps, not sovereign, after all, in the absolute. But whatever the circumstance that might have been involved with it, *her* advent certainly had plenty to do with one Desmond Drew.

Desmond Drew was an individual that qualified as being "creepy." Creepy in the sense that he had an overwhelming interest, almost a fetish, for surreptitious encounters with the darker creations of man's imagination. Whether from books, movies, or magazines, he absolutely gorged himself on the horror and terror provided by monsters, both supernatural and human. He loved Poe's pits and pendulums and Lovecraft's creeping blasphemies that haunted his decadent New England villages. His appetite for the macabre was truly insatiable; he was a veritable glutton when horror was concerned.

And it was, in fact, through a book dealing with his obsessions that he happened to first come in contact with *her.*

It all began at Desmond's own house. He had just finished reading William G. Blackmon's *Malignant Entities of the Ancient Middle East*, an encyclopedia of evil gods, goddesses and creatures arising from that part of the world, spanning the time of Gilgamesh through the conquest of Persia by Alexander the Great. Desmond was just about to close the book when he noticed on the inside of the back cover some very brilliant and beautiful scarlet script. It read:

"Is there any mortal, I wonder, who would take interest in my plight and provide me succor?"

Desmond read it, wrinkled his brow, then read it again. He studied the style of the cursive letters. It possessed such a perfect consistency and such a pleasing flourish, that it commanded admiration. It almost soothed him to study it. And never, he decided, had he seen such brilliant red ink. He guessed that it was written by a feminine hand, and this was why, in addition to the fact that he was a lonely bachelor, he suddenly, on an irresistible impulse, grabbed a pen and below the scarlet script wrote boldly, "Sure! Let me know how!" Then, becoming excited over the possibility of some kind of future romantic encounter with the individual who had written the red script, he closed the book and immediately drove to the library to return it.

The following morning, he felt rather silly about getting so excited over probably nothing more than a joke; nevertheless, following a week, he returned to the library just to see if there could indeed be anything to this. Retrieving the book in question, he turned to the back cover. And he was surprised, even flabbergasted to perceive, just below his own entry and in the same flaming red script, these words: "To succor me is to know me. To know me is first to read of me. Search for me, O precious Deliverer, in *Dechant's Truths*.

"*Dechant's Truths*?" he whispered. "Who is Dechant?"

He puzzled over this for a time, but finally admitted to himself that, in spite of his great knowledge of literature, he had never heard of this person. So, he referred to the library's catalogue. Nothing, however, under the name "Dechant" was listed. Desmond frowned, again wondering if this was not just a joke or hoax after all. Then he had an idea. He went to the reference section and found *Locton's Encyclopedia of World Writers*. And in that work he discovered the following:

"Dechant, Jean-Paul Dominique 1575–? A French occultist and writer who, in 1595, was expelled from France by Henry IV for 'unspeakable blasphemies against highest heaven.' He fled to

England, residing there for two years, and thence on to Palestine where he studied the Cabala. It was rumored that he was assassinated in Jerusalem by a certain Jewish sect reputed to have termed him 'a madman with powers terribly awesome in their potentiality.' This, however, conflicts with other records that state he escaped up the Nile in Egypt, disappearing forever somewhere south of the Sahara Desert.

"Although a prodigious writer, very little of his work has survived. Most of his manuscripts were destroyed in the year of his expulsion from his native country under personal order of the king of France. However, he composed a book concerning the occult he titled *Dechant's Truths* in England where, due to 'a detestable relationship with a certain very influential bitch in the English court,' the manuscript was translated to English and published in 1597. Of the ten copies published, one is retained by the Paris library, one by the library in St. Petersburg, one in Cambridge University, and one by Picten University. Three are contained in private libraries and the remaining three are missing."

"My God," whispered Desmond upon finishing the passage. He was wondering just what kind of guy this fellow *was*. It was like he was some kind of Aleister Crowley. It was as if he had written the *Necronomicon* or something.

"Dechant''s Truths." He whispered the name of the book over and over. This book was suddenly very interesting to him. He decided that even if there was nothing to the red script, he would like to read this particular work anyway. Obtaining it was suddenly irresistible to him. And besides, there might really be a damsel in distress out there somewhere, and if to assist her meant studying a madman's writings, so be it. He was committed.

Then, five seconds later, Desmond's eyes grew wide. He bent forward over the book in disbelief. For there, slowly becoming manifest under the words "Picten University," was a line of flaming crimson.

* * *

"But, why keep a book here if you don't let people borrow it?"

* * *

Desmond was becoming angry. After all, to reach the place in which he was now talking, he had traveled hundreds of miles in blistering summer weather in his old, rundown Dodge sedan. And it had broken down twice during this trip. Moreover, he had taken his vacation leave from the bookstore in Indianapolis, where he was employed as a clerk, thus canceling any plans he had made that year for a sojourn in Florida. Yes, he had endured and sacrificed plenty to get here, Witchdance, Connecticut, that is. For this little community was the location of Picten University. And now this little so and so snob of a head librarian, who, Desmond guessed, must think he was something really special, was not even going to let him to *see* this institution's copy of *Dechant's Truths*—much less permit him borrow it.

"Why, Mr. Kenton? Please. I drove all the way from Indiana. I won't have it long."

"I thought I had explained this to you already, Mr. Drew," replied the librarian with a thick, blue-blooded New England accent that came close to actually nauseating his listener. "Did I not state that the volume in question is priceless—that there are only seven known copies remaining in the entire world?"

"Yes, I know th—"

"And did I not also state that the use of our copy is reserved only for the students, faculty and alumni of this institution—and only then by special permission?"

"Yes, you told me that, too, but—"

"And could I be wrong here?—or have I not already informed you that the book is almost four hundred years old—that it is in delicate condition, and must be handled with extreme care?"

"Yes, yes, you told—"

"And all of this aside, what caused you to presume, Mr. Drew, that you could come here and borrow from this university such a priceless article without so much as an expressed valid reason?"

"Okay, *okay*!" Desmond cried. "I give up. Keep it. Keep it under lock and key. I won't even ask you to let me see it. But, listen, surely you have a newer edition I could borrow. Or, if not a reproduction in book form, surely you have it on microfilm. A famous book like that *must* have been reproduced in some manner."

Mr. Kenton now perceived how really desperate this person was to examine *Dechant's Truths.* But the sides of his mouth turned down even more. Then he said, "It's *not* a famous book. How long, Mr. Drew, have you known that such a book even existed? As you are employed as a clerk in a bookstore, I gather that you know literature fairly well. How many times, then, has *Dechant's Truths* been a subject in your literary discourse? If this book is so famous, as you claim, why do so many people not know of it? Let me tell you this—and you'd best believe it—there's something about this book that, down through the years, has caused any prospective publishers to purposely repress the very knowledge of its existence. They wanted nothing to do with it—in spite of any possible financial gain. Do you have any idea of the subjects it explores? I do. You see, I *have* read it. Not all of it, mind you, hardly a fourth of it. But that portion which I did read dealt with such vile, unspeakable blasphemy and malevolence that I could not finish it. I tell you I felt threatened. Aye, sucked in by extra dimensions too terrible and awesome to comprehend. I sensed dark beings, maleficent entities peering over my shoulder as I read it. I experienced malignant anticipation. I sensed them, countless numbers of them, waiting in the darker aspect of the metaphysical realm—only waiting for me to reach the point of no return. The point where they could take total possession of me, forcing me, perhaps, to commit that which was necessary to release them in this world in physical forms. I still, to this day, thank God I was able to pull away in time and cease reading the accursed thing. But the experience was not without repercussions. Even now I am troubled with nightmares because of it.

"But one thing it taught me: Everything is truly a matter of opposites. Man and woman, night and day, good and evil. I came to believe in the All Mighty because of that book; if only as a counterbalance to those evil things I felt while reading it.

"Leave it alone, Mr. Drew. Leave the damn thing alone. I would gladly let you borrow it if I knew it wasn't dangerous to do so. But Dechant was a cancer. He wrote only of the negative, and of how to give that negative the power to harm us more so than it already does. If the power were mine, I'd burn every remaining copy of the loathsome work. I've seriously considered destroying the copy here, and now I think I really shall. Yes, I think I—"

Here the librarian stopped talking. He became as stiff as a statue. Not even his eyes blinked. For he was suddenly staring at something—riveting his eyes in disbelief at something behind Desmond. The book clerk turned in the direction of the stare, and became just as motionless as Kenton.

For there on the wall, enormous and in the familiar crimson script was a message. It read, "He is a dead man, O my precious Deliverer. Remove the keys from him and unlock the container. Attain the book and behold how beautiful I am. There is nothing to fear from any who would detain you. Nor is there need to fear any lie this man has used to prevent my succor."

Desmond stared in opened-mouth awe at the huge writing plainly before him. Then a sound near the floor behind him brought his attention back to the librarian.

He found Kenton collapsed in a heap. The face was ghastly. It was ashen; it reflected extreme terror. The eyes were wide open, even bulging, and seemed quite lifeless. Kenton must had seen something else in that script—something, perhaps, mortal man should not witness.

Desmond bent over the motionless form and gently shook it, calling out his name. But there was no response. Desmond, believing the man had suffered a heart attack, rose to run for help. But he did not make it to the door. Instead, he paused and read some new script on the wall before him. It was larger and more brilliant than ever. It seemed to positively emanate an aura of rich crimson. It read, "Lend the fool to his own fate, my precious one.

Remove the keys and open the container. Attain the book and witness how beautiful I am."

Upon reading this, Desmond looked at the librarian, pondered a few seconds, then, almost before he was aware of his actions, he obeyed the writing. Like a scavenger he stooped over the body and rifled through the pockets searching for the keys. He quickly discovered them; then, almost sensing something foreign controlling him, he ran across the office floor to the large safe. He instinctively inserted the correct key in the lock, opened the door and reached for a large, ancient looking volume which, upon checking the cover, was indeed the copy of *Dechant's Truths*. Then, with the cumbersome thing tucked under his arm, he quickly retreated from the office—nonchalantly stepping over Kenton.

It was not until he had stepped out of the building into the daylight that Desmond began to understand just exactly what he was doing. An extensive list of realizations scrolled through his mind. One, he had abandoned a dead person without telling a soul; two, like a ghoul he had searched the corpse's pockets; and three, he had used the keys he had rifled from the corpse to steal a priceless artifact.

And now, with that same mentioned object—which was too large to conceal on his person—he was in plain sight outside in the daylight in the middle of the campus of the institution from which he had stolen it. He was close to panic; there were many people around. He had already quickened his stride, and when he saw two men in uniform—campus security guards—he broke out in a jog toward the parking lot. He managed to make it to his car, but as he fumbled with the keys, still fearing detection, a peculiar thing happened. Just as he opened the door, a very large, ugly and unidentified insect landed on the top of his hand—the hand clutching the book—and employed its stinger. It hurt like fire, and Desmond howled with the pain. At the same time he released the ten pounds of bound parchment from his grasp. It landed on the asphalt with pages open to the wind. But the thing, although very delicate and fragile, seemed to have somehow remained intact. He bent down and retrieved it; then, glancing around one last time to make certain the security guards had not noticed, he jumped in his vehicle and sped away.

But as he did so, his exhaust caught up page 97, which had been detached from the book on impact with the ground—and which a curious little frigid whirl of wind had blown under his car. Derrick had been too occupied rubbing his injured hand and whispering curses because of the pain to notice this. The exhaust lifted it up; then that same little frigid whirl of wind again caught it and carried it far, far away.

"If you desire to help me, first you must know me. And to know me, to behold how beautiful I am, turn, O my precious one, to leaf 96."

These were the words, in the familiar crimson script that Desmond discovered on the back of the front cover of *Dechant's Truths*.

Everything seemed alright now. Picten University was very far away from the rustic cabin in the Catskill Mountains of New York in which he now found himself. But even if the location of his theft had been just up the road, Desmond, now fully collected, probably would not have concerned himself. After all, Kenton had been the only person with which the clerk had discussed the book. And the whole business had been conducted without any appointments through secretaries or receptionists. True, he had inquired from witnesses where the library was located upon first arriving at the campus, but even this did not concern him. Indeed, he was quite calm. Understand, he sensed that something supernatural—namely the creator of the red script, whoever or whatever she was—was protecting him.

Yes, everything was okay now, including his hand. All the pain and swelling had disappeared. It was strange; there was not the slightest evidence of his being stung at all.

And so, with great anticipation and excitement over the prospect of finally gaining knowledge concerning the entity he was helping, he turned, as directed, to page 96. And when he beheld the picture that that page exhibited, measureless joy exploded all through his being. At the same time he released a lengthy, whispered "*gaaahhh.*" It was fueled by pure awe, pure delight at the personage represented in the lithograph. There was no title underneath it, but this did not concern Desmond. For he knew, knew in his soul, that *this* was a picture of the creature he was assisting. And she was absolutely captivating.

Except for luscious, flowering vines entwining about her form, she was completely uncovered. And although the lithograph was created during the Renaissance, she wasn't pictured as full-figured, as women during that period were usually portrayed. Nor was she overly slender. In short, her figure fit in perfectly between those two characteristics. The face was carved and classic—the very hand of God must have fashioned it. No female he had ever seen possessed such a wondrous, angelic countenance. The colors of the print were somewhat faded, but the picture of the creature still seemed to radiate a wonderful freshness about it. An idea of her being recently created seemed to be conveyed. In a small way, Desmond was reminded of the famous picture of Venus rising from the ocean on the half shell; but, really, even she, the goddess of love, was nothing compared to the exquisite, exotic entity represented here. All about her were cherubs blowing trumpets, extolling the divine beauty of the creature. Surely *this* was the female being described and praised in *The Song of Solomon*.

For a long while Desmond, in complete fascination stared at the print, but finally he pulled his eyes away from it to the text below. The following is what he read:

"And as to the One represented just above, I, Jean-Paul Dominique Dechant, having Knowledge of the ways of the Mind from the Physical Self, and of the Spirit from the Carnal Temple, even beyond the boundaries of Time and Space, didst behold Her just so, as She didst appear before the Event. And I called out to Her, despite the knowledge that She did not perceive me.

"'O Wondrous One,' spaketh I to Her. 'Woman from the First, Angel of the Alpha, Daughter of the Dawn: O Beauteous One, with

Flesh undefileth, hast Thou Knowledge of the Perfection in Thee? Verily doth Nefertiti of Egypt, wooed by every Prince of the World, pale to nothing next to Thee. Argive Helen, whose envied Countenance launched a Thousand Ships and caused the slaughter of countless mighty Heroes and the doom of Ilium Herself, fadeth away in comparison to Thee. And Doth Aphrodite Herself blush Crimson with Shame at Thy Vision? Aye, even Eve, Mother of Man, Daughter of God, may not claimeth Quintessence, if thou art the Measure. Verily doth the Hyacinth spring forth from whence Thou Treadeth! Surely doth the Lotus, with Delight, Weep its Nector at the Touch of Thy Hands!"

"'O Child of Paradise, who is worthy to Taste that Perfumed Essence which Exudeth from the Flesh of Thy Being? And what Man that Issueth out of the Mere Ordinariness, couldst claim Thee? Yea, Thou art Fasioned to be Marveled at, and Loved solely by that One for Whom Thou was from the First Intended.'

"'But why, O Daughter of the Dawn, didst Thou ever—'"

Here the room on the page for the large script ran out, and Desmond quickly leafed the parchment. But he discovered something amiss. The text was not a continuation of the preceding, interrupted sentence. He turned back and checked the page number, then again leafed forward. Yes, it was not there. Page 97 was missing. He then remembered dropping the book and wondered.

But he did not worry long. He soon noticed that all the words on page 98 were underlined by that familiar scarlet. And, without further hesitation, he continued on:

"...And unto that man that wouldst fain Bestow once more upon Her drifting, eager Spirit the Elements necessary for Material Sanctuary, Physical Expression, I, being a Traveler of this and other spheres, a Seeker and Revealer of the Truths not sought after and thus not heretofore revealed, now do discloseth the Formula which, by God I vow, shall summon Her and manifest Her before thee posthaste with Substance and Form."

And following this were, indeed, instructions concerning the summoning of something forth from the beyond. He found it complex and lengthy. It involved occult geometry—the drawing of a triangle within a circle contained in a pentagram. It involved astronomy and astrology, namely that cluster of stars within the constellation Taurus known as Atlas's Daughters, or the Pleiades. It involved the use of salt, earth, water and fire. It called for the recitation of curious chants and invocations.

When Desmond finished reading all that which was underscored, he leaned away from the book feeling, for the first time, trepidation about just what he was dealing with here. After all, this was pure black magic. It was pure witchcraft, and the words of Kenton, the librarian at Picten University, echoed through his mind. *"Leave it alone, Mr. Drew. Leave the damn thing alone."* He became fearful, hesitant. Sure this creature was beautiful, but exactly who or what was it? As to whether or not he truly believed that someone or something *would* come to him if he performed this incantation, there was no doubt. The many crimson scripts he had witnessed were enough to completely convince him of this. But what if this entity was evil? What if it were dangerous? Was he considering committing an act contrary to the will of God, Himself? Was he placing his very soul in jeopardy?

Desmond wavered. It seemed too dangerous, not worth the risk, and he decided to close the old book and have done with it forever.

But then that same curious, icy whirl of wind that had whisked leaf 97 away a few days ago again became manifest. It flipped the preceding page back over, then dissipated as quickly and mysteriously as it had arisen, leaving the picture of the beautiful creature once again before his eyes. And again that perfect face of a goddess, and that flawless, sensual figure filled him with fascination and delight. He again lost himself in it, becoming absolutely spellbound.

How long he remained lost in the admiration of the entity the second time, he had no idea, but eventually he heard himself whisper, "There's no way you could be evil. Just no way." And it was then that he made his decision. Fully committed, he turned page 96 over, and past missing 97, to page 98, upon which were instructions for the incantation. Then he began to prepare for it.

All in all, the preliminaries required about three hours. The geometrical figures—the tracing of which was very arduous and exacting—were drawn, with the white chalk he had procured, to the appropriate dimensions, as set forth by the book, on the wooden floor. At the angles of the equilateral triangle, he had positioned the required elementals: salt, earth, and water—contained in three mason jars. As for the fourth, and most important necessity, fire, that elemental was represented by a lit red candle, placed in the exact center of the triangle.

And then the novice picked up the heavy book and began reciting certain phrases at each point of the pentagram. And as he, with the book, make his way around the figure, he began to feel and hear something. It was that frigid whirl of wind. It spun around the circle, which was enclosed by the pentagram, but which encompassed the triangle. Nor was the flame of the candle disturbed in the least, for it whirled directly along the chalk comprising the circle, keeping the candle in an eye like a miniature hurricane.

Having finished his circuit around the pentagram, Desmond strode to the open window and searched the night sky for Taurus. He had little trouble finding it; there was no light pollution. Indeed, the night sky sparkled brilliantly with stars. Upon locating that constellation, he recited that which the book instructed at the cluster of six tiny stars within Taurus known as the Pleiades. And as he did so, the freezing, whirling wind became stronger, much stronger. He could easily hear it behind him, and now even feel it. It was an icy blast against his back. But he dared not turn around to look, for that was forbidden.

On and on he read, quite frightened, but determined to consummate the incantation. And then he was suddenly at the final stage: the concluding invocation. There was a regular tempest in the room by now, a frigid, roaring typhoon. There was frost on the window panes. He was shivering. He was struggling against the gale to keep his balance. But he persevered. Looking intently at those tiny six stars, he screamed out the final words:

> "And by the Power of that Contemplating Other Who shall be Nameless on this Sphere, and by the Power of Spirit beckoning Spirit, let Her now come forth from whence Her Essence dwelleth to join with that which She must needs clothe Herself and become once again a Breathing Entity on the Earth!"

And something did come. It first appeared as a pin prick of light slowly arching out of the Pleiades. But very quickly it became brighter and faster; and Desmond watched in awed fascination. Soon it was like a fiery meteorite. It shot down through the ether, trailing behind a flaming, crimson tail. It was as if an invisible cosmic hand wielding a colossal transparent pen was streaking a searing line of scarlet ink across the night firmament. It shot closer and closer, challenging with its flight, perhaps, the speed of light. Or was it the speed of thought itself?

And then he momentarily forgot all about everything—the spell, the goddess, the storm. This happened when he realized that the blazing comet thing was coming right towards him. He fell to the floor and prepared, as best he could, for the impact.

But there was no impact; no loud crash at all. There was just a searing *whishing* over his back as something entered the room through the window. And then the roaring pandemonium behind him climaxed. The freezing tempest became hot like a furnace, and it rose to a crescendo of roaring and howling—joined now by a sound like wild demonic laughter. Then the wild fiery storm suddenly cooled and abated.

But Desmond had not noticed any of this. He was too busy staring, with great shock, at something that had floated in on the tail of whatever had entered. It fluttered down and reattached itself, in front of Desmond's eyes, to its rightful place. It was a piece of parchment, incredibly, but evidently, the missing paper—page 97—from *Dechant's Truths.* From Connecticut to God-knew-where to New York, it had come home. It had a picture on it, like page 96, of a female entity. But *this* entity appeared quite different from the other. It was *not* so pleasing to look at.

And meanwhile, the room was permeated with a vile, suffocating, unearthly stench—like something unwholesome, alien and even extra dimensional had just emerged from cosmic sewage and entered in. And at the same time he could hear something breathing and chortling and slobbering behind him. Now on his feet again, he was too terrified to turn around to see the source of the loathsome sounds and smell; but then again, he didn't need to. For he was well aware what it looked like. The picture of it was right before his ashen, fear crazed face. He had been HAD…royally.

The eyes of the thing portrayed in this recently arrived picture were fiery red demon's orbs, glaring out pure hatred and malignancy. The teeth were huge, sharp, yellow canine fangs. Issuing from the mouth was a long, black, forked tongue, profusely dripping a noxious spittle. Patches of course black fur were prevalent over the whole creature—including the thick, freakish, muscular appendages. The hands and feet were like those of apes'—the hairy fingers and toes brandishing razor sharp black nails. The abdomen was hairless; for it was covered with shiny green scales, like those on the belly of a snake. It possessed long black teats on its four crusty breasts, and from the vagina—a furry lipped, tiny teethed sucking mouth of a leech—there dripped a nameless corruption. Multi-colored tentacles sprang from the sides of the torso, and there was an enormous glossy black, segmented tail, like that of a scorpion, curling up from behind and oozing poison from its huge stinger. It was a combination of Medusa and Scylla and the harpies and the furies and every other mythological feminine monstrosity that had ever been written about.

But there was no mythology involved here. He knew that the *it-she* was real, and right behind him. Even now he could feel the hot moist fetid breath on his neck. But despite his terror—and just before the fury muscular appendages seized him to turn him around and face that which he had summoned—he was able to read, or was allowed to read, the text below the ghastly picture. It was the continuation on the interrupted legend from page 96.

"'decideth to pit Thyself against that Function for which Thou were first Fashioned? Was it because, Thou were created from the Dew as opposed to the Rib? And didst this not also cause Thee to feel thyself better than Adam, Himself? Didst Thou thinketh the Dew Superior to the Dust? Didst Thou, then, refuseth Him Thy ordained Obedience? And didst Thou not consider this rebellion an affront to the Great Omnipotence Himself? Didst Thou not fear He wouldst exact His Own Due for this Offense?

"'O LILITH, O LILITH, Daughter of the Dawn, what Tragedy hast now befallen Thee? Hath this new Loathsome Form now Mirrored the Poison and Vindictiveness within Thee?

"'O LILITH, O LILITH, Daughter of the Dawn, what Tragedy hast now befallen Thee? Where hast Thy once unrivaled Beauty Flown? Verily God, who didst once bestow it Thee, now hast Torn it from Thee. And in the Wake didst curse Thee with this foul Mantle in its Stead. And the Day shalt surely Dawn when He will take Thee up and rend Thee Asunder, consigning Thy Spirit to the Daughters of Atlas. For Thou dost repell Him, utterly. Nor shall he suffer Thee to Suck the Blood and eat the Flesh of the Young, as is Thy Want. Neither shall He suffer Thee to Defileth for long, this Youthful Sphere.

"'Nor shall I assist Thee to regain Physical Entity, to enter again this cursed Temple; for I fear Thee Dreadfully. Knoweth I well of Thy terrible Malice. Knoweth I well that Thou wouldst just as soon Turn against the man who wouldst deliver Thee.

"'But I bid Thee Endure, O Terrible One, for Thy Day surely draweth Nigh. I shalt not Summon Thee, for I am not a Fool. But this World doth spawn Fools Aplenty; and one day Thou shalt be summoned from the Stars by one of the Greatest.'"

II
Lilith at Large

Arnold Anders loved pressure. Not the pressure from his job. Not the pressure from all the other situations life presented him. He loved the pressure received from the weight of female bodies. Ever since he could remember, this aspect had turned him on. He desired to be sat on, stood on, walked on. He recalled, as a kid, a certain movie he saw about G.I.'s and petite little geisha girls. He remembered how stiff he had become upon seeing the geishas walking on the naked backs of the soldiers with their bare feet. It was the pressure! The luscious glorious feminine *pressure*!

Arnold resided in Memphis, Tennessee, where he was employed as a shoe salesman. It was an okay job, he guessed; sometimes it could become very boring, though. Sometimes it could get downright disgusting. After all, there were certainly more pleasant things to do than attempt to fit undersized shoes on the large smelly feet of certain of his customers, who were like as not to bitch at him for suggesting they try on larger sizes. But he supposed it was all worth it; after all, many of the women he assisted were pretty Tennessee peaches, with small, easy to fit, feet.

And then one day *the* peach entered the store. Simply put, she was an absolute knockout. And she positively emanated perfection and the sensuality of woman.

Arnold, in a half daze, watched her approach him. The he saw the luscious lips move.

"Hey, honey, I need some black pumps. You know, something to match my hair?"

"Please sit down right here," he said. "I'm sure I have just the shoes you are looking for."

Then he measured her foot. It was very petite, and the nails were painted with flaming red polish. He felt the beginning of a stiff. He wanted those feet applying pressure on his body.

"Okay," he spoke, "size seven. I think we can handle that." And he rushed to the shelves to find the style of shoes she had requested.

He quickly picked out a couple of boxes containing pumps of the correct size, then, rushed back to his pretty customer. As he fitted her with one of the pumps, he suddenly—and before he knew it—asked her name.

"You may call me 'Lil,'" she answered.

"Well, Lil, do you think it would be alright if we spent some time together?" Arnold Anders, for the first time in his life, felt really bold, almost ridiculously self-confident.

And Lil apparently appreciated this boldness. She immediately responded in the affirmative. "Of course, Arnold. Why don't we make it for tonight? We'll dine in Memphis's finest. We'll have a nice steak dinner. Then, we'll go to your place. And then..." Here, Lil smiled. She did not finish the sentence, but after all, she didn't need to.

Arnold felt sugar in his stomach. He could not believe this was happening. Within fifteen minutes, he had met the most beautiful girl he had ever seen, he had successfully asked her out, and, finally, he could expect a night of heated passion with her. He was so overjoyed, in fact, that he almost forgot to finish fitting her with shoes. He slipped both pumps on her, careful to touch Lil's feet as much as possible, then asked how they felt.

"Wonderful" she replied. "I'll take them." Then she gave him her address. "Shall I expect you around seven, Arnold?"

"Seven it shall be!" he confirmed. He watched her as she took the pumps to the clerk. She paid cash, then, before exiting, she threw him a kiss. He grinned back at her like an idiot. And it never even occurred to him how she could have known his name.

"So, Lil, what exactly do you do for a living?"

Arnold and his date were on the road in his old Volkswagen driving back after a splendid meal at one of the town's swankest restaurants. They were headed for Arnold's apartment. During the repast there had been much action under the table. They had played footsie all during the meal, and now he could not wait to get this exotic creature to his house. He was going to request that she do something he had never dared to ask a girl to do before.

"Oh, you can just say that I am an 'exister,' Lil replied. "I just do what I need to do. I get by. Let's leave it at that, okay?" She seemed a bit annoyed.

"Okay, baby, I accept that answer." Arnold, although he was very curious as to how Lil made her living, did not press her in this matter. If she desired to keep it to herself, then so be it. He wanted no negative vibes to spoil the rest of the evening.

Ten minutes later they were inside his apartment. Completely naked, they were listening to classic rock and roll on the radio. Lil was sitting on the sofa; Arnold was on the floor massaging her feet. But it wasn't long before he decided it was time for a little pressure pleasure.

"Walk on my back," he said abruptly.

"Certainly, honey. Lie on your stomach."

He immediately obeyed her. Then she stepped on him and, just like a geisha, slowly treaded up and down his tense, tired back. He felt the pressure; he felt joy course though out his body.

"Oh, walk, baby, walk!"

And she continued to do as he wished.

For a few moments more he enjoyed the massage. Then he was suddenly ready for the grand event of the evening. It was time for the great climax—or the *ultimate* pressure. Without a thought as to how she might react, he asked very loudly, "Now, would you please stand on my face?"

Lil was not surprised by this request. She was matter of fact. She replied with a simple, "Certainly, baby. I'll be more than happy to. Remember, Arnold, I am here to please you in whatever manner you desire." She evidently did not consider this request curious at all.

"All right!" he exclaimed.

She then stepped off his back in order that he could turn over on his back. Next, she handed him a cushion from the sofa. He immediately placed it under his head. Then she did exactly as he requested. Extending her hands to the wall to support herself, she stepped on his face. She then proceeded to move her feet slightly to and from, alternately tightening his skin this way and that, even pinching it. But he loved it. The slight pain resulting from it was glorious. It was the grand situation. It was the full weight of her body felt on his face through the soles of her feet! It was Shangri-La. It was paradise! It was PRESSURE!

"Oh, yeah!" he cried. Do it, baby! His voice was quite smothered, but she still understood what he said.

Furiously he stroked; then he exploded down below with measureless ecstasy. A few seconds passed as he milked it for all it was worth. Then, completely fulfilled, he informed Lil that she could now step off of his face.

But Lil did *not* step off of his face. She remained steadfast where she was; for she had her own special plans for this guy. For Lil was no ordinary human being. Indeed, she really wasn't a human being at all. She was old, even ancient. And she was evil, an entity of pure malignancy. Some fool had, through magic, released her from her confines in the stars and summoned her to earth; and now she was prepared to wreak havoc on the human race. All is but illusion; and now she shed hers. She discarded the false mantle that men loved. But she hated it, because she knew that it *was* only a mantle—an agonizing reminder of the beauty she once possessed. She was ready to kill. For she was Lilith, the she-demon. Lilith: creature of the night, slayer of men, corrupter of women, abductor of children.

Arnold, meanwhile, could not see her. It was fortunate for him that he couldn't. He could not see the waving scorpion tail, the writhing tentacles; the hideous, ghastly face upon which God Himself had wrought vengeance. He could, however, hear the slobbering and the chortling. And he could also smell her; the stench was gagging, completely malodorous.

And now the thing gathered unto it all the weight of the damned. And evil is extremely ponderous.

"Ahhhh! Get off," he attempted to say, "please!" And he clutched helplessly at the ankles. He felt fur.

The thing above him laughed at his feeble struggles. Then, in a voice from hell, a raspy, cracking ungodly sound, the it-she spoke. "No way, lover. Remember, this is what you wanted me to do. Doesn't it turn you on anymore?"

The she became even heavier. Arnold could feel his facial bones bending in; and all the while, he released smothered screams.

"How do you like it?" asked the demoness. "Is this enough *pressure* for you?"

Arnold kept trying to scream. In extreme pain and terror, he felt his cheeks caving in. He felt his teeth cutting through his lips. He felt his brow give way. He felt his eyes being squashed like grapes. His whole face was collapsing under the relentless pressure. Finally, when his facial bones were crushed into his brain, it mercifully ended.

But Lilith was not quite done yet. Her toenails, which were like a preying bird's talons, now came into play. Like a chicken scratching at dirt, she raked away in the crushed skull, and sent flesh and bone flying. Finally, when the mayhem was completed to her satisfaction, and resuming her nice, attractive illusion, she wriggled her toes inside the messy gore. She loved the feeling of soft stuff between her toes. Only this soft stuff was not mud; it was brains.

"Oh, my God!" exclaimed chief detective Nick Dalton. He was studying, along with the other detectives and police, the body of what used to be a whole human being. "Jesus!" cried Dalton. "What in the world happened to this guy?"

The "guy" lay on the floor. He was fine from the neck down. But where the head should have been, there was only a bloody, brainy mess. The head was pulp. Even a Magnum .44 could not have produced such damage. The detectives, fighting back nausea, then proceeded to search the apartment for evidence. The place seemed mainly undisturbed. But they proceeded to photograph and gather any evidence they could. And this, of course, included the footprints. They discovered a trail of small naked footprints leading from the body to the open window…composed of blood. This signaled an act as perplexing as it was heinous—for the apartment was four stories up. It was as if the creator of those prints had walked to the window and simply flown away.

It had begun as an average enough day for Detective Dalton. His old detestable alarm clock had promptly aroused him at six o'clock a.m. He had then, as usual, gulped down his coffee, which seemed absolutely necessary for him to face the world and function in it. Finally, after attiring himself in one of the monkey suits he hated to wear, he drove on to work. Arriving at the police station, he was greeted, as usual, by his fellow detectives and police officers. Nothing much had seemed to be happening this morning; he hoped it would be an uneventful day in Memphis, Tennessee. Then, around eleven, a call came in from one of the apartment complexes. It seemed that one of the tenants, a guy named Arnold Anders, had not been seen or heard from for five days. Checking up on him, a friendly neighbor had knocked on his door and called out. Receiving no response, she then discovered that it was locked. The neighbor knew the subject drove a VW, and it was still parked outside. Thus, with her suspicions aroused, she decided it prudent to call the police. The cops, responding to the call, had proceeded to Anders's home. Receiving no answer to their calls and knocks, they saw fit to obtain the master key from the landlord.

Opening the door, their nostrils were immediately assailed by the pent up odor of decay; and then they saw the naked, grisly thing on the floor. They had then summoned Dalton, along with other detectives, to the scene.

"Should we dust for prints?" asked Tom Franklin, Dalton's junior associate detective.

"I suppose so," answered Nick. "But I really don't think it will help us much. I think this case will prove too unique for prints to help. But dust anyway and also, before we call the coroner and question the neighbors, chalk off the body."

During the following week, all of Memphis was buzzing about the strange, gruesome murder in Parkview Apartments. It was just too bizarre to be an average homicide. And as far as Nick Dalton was concerned, he found himself at a dead end. There were no witnesses, no leads, and the fingerprints did not help at all.

"I've got to tell you, Tom," said Dalton, a week later to his partner, "this case at Parkview has me stumped."

"Yeah, I know," replied Franklin. "It's certainly the strangest case I've ever been involved with." He paused in reflection. Then he added, "Exactly what, so far, have you deduced?"

"You know about as much as I do. It's as if a female—if you consider the small size of the footprints—scraped off his face, smashed in and tore his whole head to pieces, stepped in the mess and, well, just flew out the window."

"Strange," whispered Franklin.

"Yeah," added Dalton, "absolutely."

Two weeks after the authorities had discovered the body of Arnold Anders, Nick Dalton, sitting at his desk and mulling over the homicide, heard the phone ring. He picked up the receiver.

"Hello?"

No answer at first. So he repeated himself. "Hello?"

"H-hello? Is this Chief Detective Nick Dalton?" It was obviously a distressed voice on the other end.

"Yes, this is him. Who's speaking, please?"

"I need t-to talk with you, Detective—to meet you somewhere. It's very urgent."

"Who is this? Talk to me about what?"

"About-about the…murder of that Anders guy."

Dalton immediately perked. Maybe this could be a break in the case. "Okay, but first, I need your name."

"I'll tell you that later." The guy sounded terrified. "I just need to meet you in person somewhere."

"Okay," said Nick. "Where would you like to meet up?"

"Your place," answered the caller. "That okay?"

"Fine," Dalton responded. "You have my address on Beale Street from the phone book?

"Yes, I do. What—what time will you be home?"

"Anytime after seven-thirty PM."

"All right, I'll be there tonight." And the caller abruptly hung up.

Nick slowly replaced the receiver, wondering if this call represented a true lead. Or, he questioned himself, if it was just a crank call. "No," he whispered to himself. "The guy sounded too sincere." His mind then returned to the gory mess that had once been Arnold Ander's head; he desperately hoped that the call was legitimate. He especially did not want the perpetrator of this particular murder free on the streets.

When seven o'clock arrived, he rushed home. He didn't want to miss his caller. Seven-thirty found him sitting in his living room anxiously awaiting the visit from the mysterious guy with the frantic voice who had called him on the telephone. Nor was it long before someone showed up. When Dalton answered the knock at the door, he saw a rather diminutive, haggard man with disheveled white hair standing before him. He was obviously perturbed. His shaking hands and darting eyes gave ample evidence of this. He was holding something under his arm. Nick peered closer and perceived that it was a leather-bound, very old appearing book. And it was huge; it gave the illusion that the man who held it was smaller than he actually was.

"Come in," said the detective.

And the stranger obeyed. Once inside, he asked, "Detective Nick Dalton?"

"Yes. And you are?"

"Drew—Desmond Drew." Then he quickly asked a favor from Nick.

"Could I imposition you for some whiskey? I think you ought to pour one for yourself, too. I think that we will soon both need it."

Dalton wondered how a complete stranger could be so straightforward right off the bat. Nevertheless, he prepared two glasses of whiskey and water. Eagerly Drew took it from his host—he almost snatched it—and quickly guzzled it down. Meanwhile, Dalton, unwilling to drink good whiskey too quickly, sipped on his.

The caller, now sitting on the sofa, laid the huge book down on the coffee table. Then, still very nervous in spite of the alcohol, he began talking.

"Yes, Desmond Drew is my name. And I am a fool. Do you believe in the supernatural, Detective? If not, I think you'd better. I tell you, there are forces at work in this cosmos that would turn your hair white—as it did my own. You see, a year ago I called something down from the stars—something I thought was benign and beautiful, but which turned out to be a walking malignancy, something purely evil. But I only did it because I was lonely. I merely longed for a companion. Let me tell you my story."

And so Desmond related everything to the detective. He withheld nothing. And as strange as it might have been, Nick, notwithstanding his analytical mind, found this seemingly fantastic tale quite credible. For Nick was no stranger to supernatural happenings. In his ten years as a detective, he had, more than once, encountered things not of the mundane. He had gained a healthy respect for Voodoo and the like when he was on the New Orleans police force. And in one of the old, supposedly haunted houses in Memphis, he had once seen something that he swore to himself was indeed a genuine ghost. So he listened to the speaker with an open mind.

And then Drew got into the subject of the relic he had brought with him.

"This thing," he said, pointing to the book, "is called *Dechant's Truths.* It is what helped me to release her from her prison and call her down to earth for me. But you have to believe me Detective Dalton; I only did it because, as I mentioned, I was desperate for a companion. But this cursed book fooled me into believing that the entity I summoned by it would be lovely and wonderful. But the thing is horrid—and evil beyond words. You've heard of Lilith, Adam's first wife? Well that is who—*what* it is. That is what I called—with the help of this accursed volume—down from the stars. And once she arrived, she made me come down South with her—to the Bible Belt. For she's anti-god. She's killed, Mr. Dalton. She loves to kill men in fiendish ways. Yes, she killed that guy, Anders—whose murder you're investigating right now. She tells me all about her heinous activities, the men she kills, the women she corrupts, the children she steals and devours. And sometimes she forces me to aid her in her vile acts. As I said, she eats children. Even now she is away preying on the young. But she'll be back, rest assured. And she'll eventually finish me, Mr. Dalton—this I know. There is no hope for me. But maybe you can send it back, Detective. You've got to expel her from the earth. I would try if I could, but, according to the book, the person who summoned her has no power to exorcise her. Someone else must do it. And this is why I came to you—and brought this book with me; for, as evil as it is, it contains a spell to send her back where she came from. You'll find the proper incantation on page ninety-nine. But you will not be able to do it alone; you will, in addition, need the services of a rabbi.

"And now I must leave. I won't survive much longer. I don't think the creature's all-knowing, thank God, but I swear that she somehow always knows where *I* am and what I do, anyway."

And then Drew broke down completely. He seized Dalton's sleeve. "Please, Detective, *please*! You've got to stop her. It intends to bring about the fall of all mankind. The fate of the very planet rests in your hands!"

Desmond Drew then arose to leave, his face showing hopeless resignation—as if he knew himself to be a doomed man. But before he walked out the door, he turned to Nick and spoke some final words:

"Don't forget: turn to page ninety-nine. That's where you'll find how to exorcize this cancer from the world. And now I must return to the creature. I'm dead and damned; I know she'll finish me. But it is only my own fault. I brought this on myself. Good luck, Detective Dalton, and farewell."

Then Drew left, leaving his troubled host puzzling over the events of the last half hour or so. It was certainly the strangest visit he had ever received. Was this wild story really true? He then looked at the huge book on the coffee table. In spite of its antiquity, it did not appear to be very worn. He opened it up; and immediately felt something odd and unpleasant deep within him. Was it his imagination, or did he *really* sense some invisible something peering at him with great anticipation and wicked intent? Something from, perhaps, a different dimension, the veil of which now seemed quite thin. He felt as though in a vacuum, as if something wicked desired to suck him in and carry him away to hell. And he shuddered. He reflected that maybe the thing was in such good condition due to a reluctance of people through the ages to peruse through very many of its forbidding pages. Maybe the would-be readers had experienced the same negative sensations from it that he had felt, and thus spared most of the pages from becoming dog-eared and stained and wrinkled with use.

But Nick was a very brave man, and he looked through the book. The text seemed to be old English, and the pages were full of diagrams, symbols, runes, and pictures—pictures of terrible, fabulous beings. Some were pictured as hiding in wait for unsuspecting wayfarers. Others were shown torturing their victims in particularly fiendish manners. Still others were shown devouring their human prey alive.

"Jesus Christ!" he whispered. And he wondered just what sort of person had written and illustrated this thing. Just who the hell *was* this Dechant fellow? Then he recalled the page he had been instructed by Drew to refer to. But, upon leafing through to the designated page, he saw page ninety-seven; and he gasped. For he saw portrayed there one of the most disgusting, vile things he had ever seen. It was all fur, fangs, talons and tentacles. It possessed a long, glossy black scorpion tail that curled up from behind the creature and dripped what was certainly poison from its hideous stinger. He studied the picture for a long time; then he turned the page. It contained the incantation for bringing this horrible thing to earth. And the hair on his neck tingled. Then he turned to page ninety-nine, and read the following:

"And unto that One upon which the Task falls to Deliver the Sphere from the great It-She, Lilith, heedeth these Words. Seek thee out a Levite. Thou must also obtain Nun, the Slayer of Mighty Men. Then, on a Night when the Moon shedeth not Her Light, when She covereth Her Face from man in the Absolute, adjoureth thou, the Levite, to Cause Flames from Wood of the Oak, the Elm and the Ash to waft to the Sky. But he must needs be alone. Thou must taketh Pains to withhold thy Presence for a Time. But when the Night Approacheth the Zenith—aye, five minutes before the Hands on the Mechanism meet and Pointeth to God, tarryeth thee not, but Repair to the Flames post haste; for verily the One called Lilith draweth nigh. For the Aroma of the Burning Wood of these Three Special Trees doth Please Her and Beckons Her. Get thee to the Source of the Flames; and when thou beholdeth Her enter in, Thrust Nun, Sword of David, King of Israel, deep within Her Dark Heart. It is only in this Manner that She mighteth be Dispached. And mindeth thee: If the One called Lilith doth, at any time, obtain the better of thee, thou mayeth seize, if only for the Instant, the Upper Hand. Stayeth not thine hand from that Place on Her Being where She is Susceptible. Flincheth thee not, but Claspeth thou Her Vulnerability, Her Special Place with all the Strength thou canst Summon; for verily shalt this Act, if only for a small Measure of Time, Deliver thee from Her Hand."

Nick, upon finishing this passage, took a deep breath. He wondered how he had gotten himself into this. He thought long and hard. Was this really to be believed? Yes, he had had encounters with the supernatural before, but *this* just seemed to be too wild, too incredulous to be taken seriously. And how in God's name would he be able to acquire the sword of David? Did it even exist? What was it called? Oh, yes, "Nun." He had never heard of it; it certainly wasn't mentioned in the Bible. He thought some more. *This guy Drew must be a lunatic,* he reasoned. Such things just couldn't be. And so Nick determined to try to put this Lilith business from his mind and approach Anders's murder as any other. Actually, however, deep in his being he knew that he *did* believe Drew's tale.

And, a few days later, the person or thing called Lilith was very much in Nick's mind again. For at the police station, he heard of three children kidnapped in northern Mississippi—with no clues as to the abductor. And he also received another homicide assignment. Some guy had been killed in a very gruesome manner. He had been decapitated. His head was found in the commode in his home. But it had not been cleanly severed. From the ragged tears in the neck, the police had concluded that the head had been literally twisted off. Something very heinous, and very strong, was at large. And the victim's name, incidentally, was Desmond Drew.

III
Confrontation

Rabbi Asher First was an old man with a magnificent white beard and full, flowing hair. He was a respected man, with much influence. People listened when Rabbi First spoke, for he was very knowledgeable. He had been around. But the rabbi was not a happy man. He was filled with too many sad and terrible memories, mainly of his confinement, as a young lad, in Auschwitz. He had suffered countless indignities there; he had witnessed thousands of people, including his whole family, gassed. He could never forget the sight and smell of the sad smoke that constantly billowed out of the crematoriums at the camp. He had witnessed his people worked or tortured to death. He remembered the pathetic screams, the pleading arms, the tearful eyes. And one of his worst memories was of the old man being nailed to the wall of one of the camp buildings. The dotard's groans of agony, his pleading in vain for the sadists who had committed the act to shoot him and release him from life especially haunted him. No, the rabbi was not a happy man; he knew that if his tragic experiences had dispelled his belief in the existence of God, he would have done away with himself long ago. For the human brain, after all, can only tolerate just so much memory of horror and pain. And although, toward the end of the war, the Russians had entered the camp and liberated his body, his mind would forever still be imprisoned in Auschwitz.

But the rabbi still managed to radiate good will to everyone he knew. Some people, having suffered great hurt or heartache seek only to cause that same hurt in people. Other victims of great pain and humiliation, however, would not dream of intentionally causing hurt. For they persist in loving people. Asher belonged to this second group of persons; he lived to love God and all people, Jew and Gentile alike, and that was why everyone he knew loved him also.

One Sabbath, as the service in Asher's synagogue was concluding, the good rabbi found himself wondering who the stranger was attending the service. He didn't appear to belong there. Was he interested in converting to the Jewish faith? Or could he just be a curious participant? He certainly seemed to be listening carefully to the scriptures the rabbi read from the Talmud. And so Asher, before the service ended, decided he desired to meet him.

But when it was over, it was the stranger who approached the rabbi. It was chief detective Dalton. He presented his credentials, then told the rabbi a very strange, lengthy story. It concerned the occult. It concerned murder. It concerned a blasphemous monstrosity that needed to be sent back to where it had originated. It was a plea for the rabbi's assistance.

The good rabbi listened intently to the detective's story. When Nick had finished, Asher nodded his head; then, with a slight Slavic accent, he spoke:

"Ah, yes…Lilith, the demon creature of the night. The one who was created by God to be Adam's wife, but who refused to be submissive to him—and was cursed by God for rebellion. I must confess, I once had doubts as to whether she really existed—just as I once questioned the existence of God, Himself; but now, having heard your tale, I am convinced of her reality. Yes, I shall help you, Detective Dalton. And we should exorcise her from the earth with all haste; for the longer she remains on the planet, the stronger she becomes. What is your plan?"

Nick then explained the procedure as laid out in *Dechant's Truths.*

"But, to expel her," added Nick, "we must have the sword of David. Even if it exists, I have no idea where it is."

The rabbi displayed no concern. "Don't worry; it, indeed, does exist—and I know where. There is a secret society, Detective, called The Greater Zion Essenes. This sect has been in existence for centuries. In fact, it was this order who supposedly assassinated this man, Dechant. They have been charged with the possession and protection of the sword. They are headquartered in Jerusalem. I shall contact them to request they lend me the relic. They won't refuse; for they know about Lilith and such matters. They are a knowledgeable society, well versed in the cabala. I shall contact them forthwith. We shall have the weapon before the next new moon."

"I hope so. Now, do you have a fireplace in your home?"

"Yes, in fact, I do"

"Good. Remember, you must build the fire all by yourself. And, keep in mind, you must use *only* the three types of wood I mentioned. Five minutes before midnight, when the thing is due to arrive, I shall come with the sword. And I mean to drive it in the heart as hard as I can. We'll send the thing back to where ever it came from. You will inform me, Rabbi First, when you obtain the sword?"

"I won't need to. It shall be delivered to you, personally."

"Let's hope it arrives before the new moon, ten days from now."

"Don't worry, it shall. And meanwhile, I shall pray to God for His help. I suggest, Detective Dalton, that you do the same."

New moon. It was eleven p.m., on Friday. And Rabbi First put the match to the logs of oak, elm and ash in his fireplace. It caught on quickly, as if something magical, or even divine, had lent a helping hand in this business. Asher sat back and watched the dancing flames, anxiously watching the clock above the mantle and awaiting the arrival of Detective Dalton. The rabbi was certainly no coward; but was, none the less, quite apprehensive. But, then, who wouldn't have been? After all, he expected, in a short while, to encounter nothing less than Evil Incarnate.

And meanwhile, five miles away, Nick Dalton prepared to leave his home and drive to Asher' house. Like the rabbi, he was prepared for meeting the she-beast. He had King David's sword, "Nun," ready at hand. Yes, it had arrived, two days ago, by a special carrier. The man had said very little. When Nick had answered his knocks on the door, he had simply handed the detective the sword and sheath. The articles were unwrapped. Then, after saying "God give you strength," the man had immediately turned and left. And "Nun," far from being the elaborate, jewel encrusted weapon he expected was plain and simple. And it was grimy and rusty—rusty, perhaps, from the blood of the "tens of thousands" the royal wielder of this weapon had, according to scripture, dispatched. But as long as it accomplished the job, Nick didn't care what it looked like. And, now, with this weapon in his hand, he kept careful eyes on his watch. He steeled himself, as best he could, for the task that lay before him.

And then the time arrived, eleven-thirty, for him to leave. With the king's sword in hand, he entered his old Mustang and drove off. He simply could not be late; that would mean disaster for the old man. But then he heard a loud, clicking sound in the car. And he began to lose power. Dalton knew what it was; it was the belts. And he cursed himself; for he had been warned earlier about them from his mechanic. He had fully intended to have new ones installed; now, however, it was too late. With another curse, he applied the brakes, turned off the ignition and got out of the car. He did not have a radio in the vehicle, for it was his personal car. Nor did he expect to hitch a ride. It was, after all, a lonely road; and, besides, people driving at night in that part of Memphis were very unlikely to stop and assist any pedestrian who signaled for a ride—especially one wielding a weapon. And so he had no choice but to run. And as he trotted, he hoped, he prayed, that he would arrive at the rabbi's house in time. But it was already twenty 'til twelve; and he had a long way to go.

Meanwhile, the rabbi anxiously watched his clock, wondering where the detective was. He thought of confronting the creature by himself—and shuddered. Helpless to do anything else, he prayed to God. And all the while, the clock kept ticking—the hands inching ever closer to twelve. Eventually both hands were almost joined. And the rabbi's clock, by the way, was, to his ignorance, three minutes slow. For checking that the clock was set to accurate time, notwithstanding the importance of the act, was somehow forgotten in all of the anticipation of the coming events.

Then, there came a clamoring at the door. Someone was knocking very loudly—practically beating the wood. Thinking that Dalton had finally arrived, the rabbi breathed a sigh of relief. He went to the door…he opened it…he saw her.

The thing had resumed the illusion again. It again portrayed a human. But this "human" was dressed up like an S.S. officer—complete with the smart but foreboding black uniform with the white trim, the high black boots and a riding crop. The cap, showing above the brim the silver death's head, was tilted at an angle on her head. And under it she was smiling. But it was a dreadful, cruel smile. It was the same smile that he often times witnessed on the faces of the sadistic guards in the death camp at Auschwitz.

Then the thing spoke. "Well, Rabbi, I am very pleased to meet you. I love meeting holy men; they are so fragile." The thing used a mocking, German accent in its speech. Then it placed the crop under his chin and tilted his head way back. "I have something very special planned for you, Rabbi. Something you should remember very well from the good old days." And it slowly reached for him.

A while later, Nick Dalton, sucking in wind, finally made it to Asher's home. But it was now well past midnight. As he approached the house, he could discern no lights inside. Knowing he was late, and fearing the worst, he knocked on the door…no answer. So he slowly opened it.

"Rabbi First!"

No answer. But the detective knew that someone or something was there. For he heard tortured groans and labored breathing. He felt for and found the light switch. He turned on the lights. He saw the Rabbi. He was nailed to a wall through his wrists and feet. Crucified. The old man was physically experiencing the event forming his worst memory.

"Rabbi!" yelled Dalton.

The old man opened his eyes. "It's here!" he managed to scream. "Behind you! Look out!"

And Nick again heard hard breathing—this time behind him. He felt hot breath on his neck. He smelled something: rotting fish, sewage, putrescence. He turned around. He saw it.

Yes, he saw it. It had cast aside the illusion. It revealed its true self. Nick beheld the result of God's vengeance personified. He saw the coarse fur, the waving tentacles, the fangs, the talons, the scorpion tail, the horrid genitalia.

"Ah, Detective Dalton; you are well met." The voice was less pleasant than fingernails scraping blackboards. "Did you really think you could hurt me with this plaything you brought?"

For an eternal moment, Nick was frozen. The sight, sound and smell of the walking blasphemy before him seemed just too unreal. Then, he remembered that he was armed. He again became aware of "Nun." And with this awareness, he suddenly sprang forward and lifted the weapon high, intending to thrust it in the heart of the thing. But Lilith was too quick for him. With her left hand, the it-she arrested his arm before he could drive the sword home. Then she seized him by the throat with her other hand and pushed him backwards against the wall. Then, with her strong, ape-like hand squeezing his throat, the thing lifted him up against the wall. And Nick, his legs dangling, was gasping for air. His windpipe was being crushed.

"And now I'm going to take you to a very special place," said the creature. "I'm sure you've heard of it. It's called hell." And it cackled like a banshee.

Nick thought it was all over for him. He could no longer breathe at all. Dancing stars appeared in his vision. He felt his eyes bulging from the pressure.

"Yes," the thing laughed, "you're going to hell—my own special place!"

Special place. Nick remembered now. Something in that book about a "special place" on the thing's body that would render it, if only for a moment, powerless.

For exactly three seconds, he wondered where this special place could be. Then, with his free left hand—and on desperate, blind instinct—he suddenly reached forward and seized one of the creature's four, horrid breasts. Then, as hard as he could, he squeezed.

The sound that then burst out of the she-demon's throat was earsplitting. Like one hundred wailing sirens, it howled with pain. A noxious, black substance gushed out all over Nick's hand. And it burned; it hurt like fire. But he had succeeded, at least temporarily, in his objective. The thing immediately released Nick and grabbed with both its hands his left arm and pulled it away from where he clutched it.

Nick's right hand, which still wielded the king's sword, was now also free. The thing had released it. Nor did he hesitate. With all of his might, he plunged the weapon deep into the thing's heart.

And again the thing screamed—louder than the first time. Nick wondered if his eardrums had burst. And then, just like that, the thing called Lilith, the mighty she-creature of the night, the slayer of men, corrupter of women and abductor of children, began to fade before his eyes. She simply began to disintegrate. She became translucent, then almost completely transparent. Soon there was nothing left but a red glowing apparition, with fiery orbs glaring pure hate. Nick then heard "Nun" hit the floor, for no substance remained to hold it in place. Finally, with one last howl, the thing, now a glowing ball of fire, rushed out of the window. It was being drawn back to where it had issued: to the Daughters of Atlas, the Pleiades, in the constellation Taurus. And as it shot up into the night sky, it trailed behind the same brilliant, glittering tail that had followed it when it was first summoned by Desmond Drew.

Nick watched the tail slowly fade away, then he turned his attention to Asher First. He found the rabbi on the floor, shaken, but otherwise unharmed. For his wounds, as well as the spikes that had pinned him to the wall, had, like Lilith, disappeared.

Neither the detective nor the Rabbi ever mentioned the horrific adventure they had experienced. They had saved untold numbers from doom, but they were both modest men—neither one desired glory or fame. And even if the contrary were true, who would have believed their story anyway? They were just relieved that they had successfully completed their task. Lilith had been expelled from the earth.

But if they had known the *entire* truth of the story, they probably would not have felt relieved at all. For Desmond Drew had not *quite* related everything to Nick about his relationship with the night creature. He had not mentioned another female thing down in Haiti. A terrible thing under the care of certain ambitious and evil people. A malignant thing that had suckled black milk from crusty breasts. It was a small, writhing, howling, frightful thing fathered by a fool and mothered by the nightmare that this fool had summoned down to earth out of the Pleiades.

ANAVRIN

Sidney J. Shannon was, without question, the cruelest, most wicked and vindictive person I had ever known. Being the wealthiest, most powerful person living in Witchdance, Connecticut, Sidney J. Shannon dealt unmercifully with anyone who, whether real or imagined, he sensed was a threat to his paramount status in the town. He was the owner and president of Shannon Steel Inc., and he enjoyed squashing any potential competitors like insects. Nor were his schemes and machinations confined to the steel business alone, for Sidney J. Shannon plotted against any enterprise that he feared would become more profitable than his own. He was preoccupied with having more money and influence than any other person in the town, and because he owned the mayor, the town council, the police chief and all the others in high places, this obsession was realized. He practically held a stranglehold over the town, and because of this, Witchdance remained, for the most part, unprosperous and stagnant.

Picten University was our main redeeming aspect. He had not meddled as yet in this institution, mainly because he perceived no threat there to his authority. Even so, he often attended our seminars—probably just to remind the faculty, students and intellectuals in Witchdance who was boss. And, although I knew of him—as did everyone in town—it was at one of these seminars that I met him personally.

I was a professor of metaphysics and parapsychology at this university, and, following one of my lectures, he approached me, expressing a strong curiosity in my field of study. We talked for a while, and then, he even invited me to dine with him later that evening at his home.

It should come as no surprise that when a man like Sidney J. Shannon was concerned, true companionship did not exist. He did have certain acquaintances, of course, but all of them, without exception, were mere yes-men and sycophants. As it turned out, I became the only person in Witchdance that could qualify as being a genuine friend to him. But I use the word "friend" loosely. The relationship that developed between us turned out, at best, tenuous. And although this "friendship" was, at times, difficult to maintain—I experienced no little distress during this relationship—I did not desert him right away. That only happened later, when the last bit of hope and respect I had reserved for him had completely dissolved.

I suppose the main reason I endured this person for so long was that Sidney J. Shannon intrigued me. It was not, after all, so much that I desired to be a true friend to him. It was mainly because I sought to discover some quality about this man that was not based wholly on cruelty, selfishness and aggrandizement. Surely there was something good about this individual. No person's spirit, I believed, was totally dark; no essence completely hopeless. Certainly something decent—if just a tiny spark of benevolence—resided in his soul. And it was this hidden spark that I wanted to finally see displayed in him. And so I spent time with Shannon—and endured his special kind of abuse in waiting to witness it.

Now, it should also be noted that, in spite of his many negative characteristics, he *was* a knowledgeable individual; and, perhaps, I thought I could actually learn something from him that could be of benefit to me. Anyway, I have no doubt but that *this* was why he desired my own company. I certainly didn't think he actually liked me.

Looking back, I recall how he would frequently, during our conversations, slip in subtle insults and sly putdowns. For some reason, which I to this day do not understand, he resented me. He desired to constantly bait me. And he was always successful in this, for I always retaliated. Yes, I swapped insult for insult. It was like an adult version of two children calling each other names. And he loved to challenge me with mind games. I detested this fervently. I looked upon it as entirely unproductive, even stupid; but I always joined in with my own indulgence in these mental jousts. And I suppose that he always felt victorious in these silly activities. I say this because it was always I who signaled a desire to change the subject of whatever we were "discussing." Such then, was the nature of our association, our "friendship."

For a year or thereabout, this relationship between Shannon and me continued pretty much unchanged. Then came the night when he dined with the Indian from Calcutta. This man—Mahendra was his name—was a worldwide respected metaphysician and mystic. Touring and lecturing across the United States, he was invited by Picten University to speak at that institution. Shannon attended his lecture, and, suddenly deciding that he wished to know more about Eastern philosophy and mind states, he invited the Indian to his residence for dinner, just as he had once invited me. I suppose Shannon, tiring of my own conjectures and theories on metaphysics and parapsychology, wanted a new, different perspective on these subjects. At any rate, he and the visitor must have found each other agreeable, for Mahendra postponed his travels in favor of staying indefinitely at Shannon's mansion. Then, following a month or so, Shannon surprised the whole town by suddenly leaving with the Eastern teacher for an extended stay in India.

Nor did he correspond with anyone while he was away—not even with me, who was the closest thing to a friend he had in town. It was as though he had just vanished. He probably did not miss Witchdance, and Witchdance, I am sure, did not miss him. His absence was like a relief; it was truly appreciated. For the first time in years, our community experienced true freedom. It was as if the town bully had moved away.

But, as it turned out, Shannon had not departed for good. The day arrived, about six months later, when he returned as unexpectedly as he had left. I was the first one to know of his arrival; he called me immediately upon his return. He had very few words to say over the phone. He simply asked—no, demanded—me over, claiming he had something of great importance to show me.

"Tell me, Williams, what do you think you *really* understand about metaphysics?"

This was the question with which Shannon immediately challenged me upon my arrival at his residence. And, after directing me to sit down in a chair in his study, he continued his examination.

"Ontology, cosmology, parapsychology,—what do you presume you *actually* know about these sciences? You claim to be a metaphysician and a parapsychologist. Then, tell me, you pretender, what *is* the ultimate nature of things?"

It was not the subject of these particular questions that caused me to hesitate before attempting to answer him. We had, after all, discussed these matters before. Rather, it was the especially obnoxious, intimidating manner in which they were presented to me. He was practically calling me a fool. It was almost as if he wanted to slap me in the face. I thought that I knew him fairly well, but this new form of spite left me momentarily speechless.

As I gathered myself together to respond, I saw him smirk. It was an ugly, knowing smirk. It reflected, possibly, an idea in his mind that he knew some great secret; something to which only he was privy. It was like he now considered himself the most enlightened person in the world. This sent a wave of anger through me. I had not been there five minutes, and already I had had enough.

"I think that I *really* know a good bit about the ultimate nature of things," I snapped back. "At least I know enough about it to make a decent living. In fact, I'll wager you, Shannon, that I know more about metaphysical theory than you."

"That's your problem, Williams," he replied. "You base your knowledge on mere theory and conjecture. You consider pure facts and logic as unimportant. And that's why you are quite pathetic. You grasp at straws. Tell me, Williams, do you look upon the existence of God as theory or fact?"

"What are you driving at, Shannon?" I angrily demanded. "You already know how I feel about that. What are you really asking?"

"You teach metaphysics. Metaphysics includes the subject of supernatural phenomena, does it not? You know…God, Divine

Logic and such. And Divine Logic includes the concept of karma. Tell me, Williams, what do you presume to really know about karma?" He asked this last question with a triumphant air.

"Everyone knows what karma is, Shannon," I answered, "but if you want an interpretation, I'll provide you one. It's the force that determines how well one fares during the reincarnation process. It's based on the thoughts and actions of each preceding life."

"Very *good,* Williams! Very good. But do you know how many times a person must be reborn in mortal form until he escapes the Karmic Wheel of Life? Do you have any idea how many lives one must endure before he earns the pure, perfect existence? The amount is both astounding and distressing. It is barely finite."

Here Shannon paused and again showed me that sneer. Next he opened a safe in the wall and brought forth from it a small, ornately decorated vial. With that detestable smirk still plastered on his face, he gazed at the small container as if he held the Hope diamond in his hand. Then he continued talking.

"But what would you think if I said that there is a much quicker, easier way? What would you think if I told you that I've found a short cut through karma to God?"

"I would think that you had been duped," I answered, "or that you were completely insane."

"Open your mind, damn you!" he was practically screaming. "Do you know that it is a *fact* that a certain well in Trivandurm in India contains water so pure that it possesses mystical qualities capable of bestowing the imbiber immortality? Do you know that it is a *fact* that there exists on this planet a vessel containing dust from the star of Shiva? Do you know that it is a *fact* that the god Vishnu once purposely pricked his finger—to shed three drops of his essence for the virgin maidens of Jaunpur? The water, the dust, the essence: this vial contains a portion of all three. It represents escape from the karmic wheel, Williams. It is instant nirvana!"

And then Shannon began to relate the adventures he had experienced with Mahendra in India. And it was replete with treachery, deceit, and even murder. He recounted with glee the way he had betrayed his Indian companion to obtain the vial. He laughed maliciously as he related how he had Mahendra garroted by an assassin. Listening to him, I found myself alternating between shock and disgust. He was finally revealing how truly, how hopelessly malignant he was. It caused me to finally realize that I needed to end my relationship with him. I decided that I could no longer associate with someone so completely void of honor and conscience. That spark of decency I had looked for in him simply did not exist.

I waited until he had finished his story, then I very bluntly informed him of the new situation between us. I told him flatly that he was, from that moment on, to consider our association terminated. I did not explain why, and if he did not understand my decision, I felt that it was the fault of his own. Then, without a farewell gesture, I left his house. But this was not without parting shots from the man. As I was leaving through the door, I heard Shannon exclaim how much he welcomed being disassociated with "such a fool." And this was accentuated with insults and obscenities that need not be recorded.

When I left Shannon's house that night, I felt sure that I would never communicate with him again. And during the month or so that followed, I experienced feelings of relief, even freedom. I also felt foolish, for enduring such a negative relationship for so long a time. But I determined not to let this bother me. I decided to put forth my all into my professorship—the quality of my lectures had deteriorated during my relationship with Shannon—and try to forget about the man.

But, as it turned out, my association with Shannon was not quite concluded. For the evening arrived when he called me on the phone. His voice was frantic. He claimed that he was experiencing something horrendous, and he asked me to come to see him with all haste. I was the only person he claimed he could turn to. At first, I refused. After all the man had become absolutely odious to me. But he implored. He literally begged me to come, and so desperate and pitiful were his entreaties, that I finally gave in and agreed to see him. Driving over, I wondered what on earth had happened to him. For to hear the wealthy, the powerful, the self-assured Sidney J. Shannon beg for anything was unheard of.

Upon arriving at his residence, I departed my car and headed for the door. And as I walked to the entrance, I heard loud screams from within the mansion, and I shuddered. It sounded like the howls of someone whose very soul was in torment. But I did not hesitate. Without knocking, I went to the living room. And there I was greeted with a shocking, unreal sight. I witnessed Shannon in his bed trousers lying on the sofa, his naked stomach grotesquely swollen. It was immense; it resembled a pregnant woman's abdomen—only it protruded out much more. I wondered why his skin had not ripped open. Then I could see the movement. Bumpy impressions were furiously arising and subsiding in the skin along the surface. It was as though his guts were boiling. And I stood transfixed in absolute disbelief at what I was seeing.

Shannon, meanwhile, continued to scream. He was in obvious agony. But when he saw me, he managed to speak.

"I shouldn't have tried it, Williams! I should never have drank that substance! That damned potion! I can feel it! I can feel it all over—in my stomach, my chest, my head! I feel it sucking! Do something, Williams! It's sucking down my mind!"

I do not know how long I stood paralyzed in mute shock. Nor could I think of any possible way I could render him assistance. But I was finally able to ask him what was happening to him.

"Karma! It's karma, Williams! I thought I could pass it over. I thought it could be cheated. But there is no escape from karma. The stuff in the vial is only for the damned! It is only for those who presume karma can be trifled with, can be cheated! It's the cosmic joke! The wheel turns! There's no escape from karma!" And again he shrieked in horrible agony.

Unable to think of anything else to say, I asked him if he wanted a doctor.

"No doctor can help me! No one can help me. I *feel* it! It's sucking down my mind. It's eating my soul! But it's me! It's *me*! Don't you understand, Williams? It's karma! It's *me* a million years from now!"

Then he vented a final, climatic scream. This was accompanied by muffled, tearing sounds from his abdomen. It sounded like something ripping through leather. Then, as I continued to watch, my eyes transfixed on his stomach, I suddenly witnessed a thick, oily vapor shoot forth from it. It was like black steam. The room was then suffused with the most noxious odor that had ever assailed my nostrils, and I gagged. Meanwhile the dark steamy emission was taking on a certain form. I witnessed it manifest itself into something solid. Something that breathed. Something that would cause me nightmares thenceforth. I shall not attempt to describe what the thing looked like, for I do not wish to trouble the reader's sleep as well. I will, however, state that it was monstrous beyond imagination. It wriggled, it writhed. It hissed and howled—and stank like Gehenna. And the only feature it possessed that I will mention was its frightful one eye—a cephalopodan monstrosity that moved anywhere on the thing's body that it pleased to place it. Then the thing, now floating above Shannon, began to destroy his body. I saw it claw viciously into his flesh. I saw it ripping him to pieces—and flinging the gore all about the room.

And that was enough for me. I managed to free myself from the trance that had seized me and flee from that place. Even today, I believe that if I had remained longer, I would have lost my mind.

But as it was, my terror was not over. For just before I escaped out of that terrible room, I heard one final sound. It was an unearthly, gurgling noise. I know that it emanated from that nameless thing that had torn out of Shannon. And I swear I think it was trying to sound my name.

The authorities were utterly baffled when what remained of Shannon was discovered. They investigated the case as thoroughly as possible, but, of course, their endeavors yielded nothing. As for myself, I remained silent. Even though I knew the strange, entire truth, I decided not to come forward with the information. It was just too fantastic a story, and I had my position at the university to consider. So I said nothing, and in the end, the police, as lame as it was, ended up attributing his destruction to a rabid bear or some other mad creature. No human, they reasoned, not even the most homicidal, could have caused such mayhem.

There is one last thing. Around a year following the grisly event I witnessed in Shannon's living room, I read in the paper about the disappearance of a teenage boy who had been fishing in the nearby Shetucket River. According to his companions, a "monster with a big eye" had grabbed the victim and pulled him down into the water. For a long time there was talk around Witchdance about this incident. Many theories and conjectures concerning the disappearance were discussed, but, of course, no one really knew the truth behind the abduction. No one but me. I knew it all too well. *It* had become hungry. *It* had captured a meal. *It* was the result of countless reincarnated stages sped through in a few moments. *It* was a hopelessly evil man degenerated and physically evolved through karma to his last and loathsome perfect state. *It* was the final true evil, unrepentant essence of Sidney J. Shannon. *It* was a personification of the damned state of Anavrin—the terrible, dark opposite of Nirvana.

PINE TREES

Clifton had a problem with pine trees. To say that he did not care very much for them would be quite the understatement. The truth was that he despised pine trees. It might have had something to do with his mental condition. "Slightly schizophrenic" was his psychiatrist's diagnosis. But Clifton would probably have denied that his illness had anything to do with his negative feelings toward these conifers. And this was because when he experienced his loathing of the trees, he felt completely sane, rational, and justified.

Clifton wondered how anyone could like pine trees. Didn't they realize the truth about them? Did they not know that these trees were nothing more than big weeds ruining the potential beauty of any area of land that supported them? They were just plain ugly. First of all, they didn't present a nice rounded crown like many of the deciduous trees did. They didn't spread out into the pleasing, tapering limbs typical of oaks, elms and others. No. Instead, pine trees had trunks that reached all the way from the bottom to the top, with the branches sticking out unattractively all around. And they didn't present the nice broad leaves on their branches like the hardwoods. No. Instead, they sported those unappealing growths called needles. Pine needles—which, unlike the leaves of hardwoods, remained the same drab green color in the autumn. Pine needles—which, when shed, became pine *straw.* Pine straw—dirty brown looking shit that covered the ground, forcing one to eventually rake it into mounds and burn it. And, God, how it stank when it burned! And the pine cones! He really hated the pine cones. To him they were just some kind of unsightly, useless growths, littering the ground when they fell and forcing a barefoot person to watch his step. Clifton had stepped on more than a few in his time, and it hurt. Nothing was good to him about these trees. Even the coarse, scaly bark they presented was a turn off to him. And it didn't matter what species of pines they were. Whether they were short leaf, long leaf, loblolly, pitch, or whatever, he despised them all.

And what really pissed him off was their prolific rate of reproduction. In southeast Alabama, where he lived, they seemed to be everywhere. They crowded the roadsides and took over the fields. They seemed to shoot up in no time. And in the springtime, the yellow pollen from the adults covered everything, playing havoc with his nose and eyes.

Pine trees! As a kid, you couldn't have fun climbing them because you always got that sticky resin stuff all over your body. And as for building a tree house in them, you could forget it. Never in recorded history, as far as Clifton was aware, was there a single instance of a tree house built in a pine tree. They simply were not suitable for tree house construction. *Pine trees!* You couldn't cook over the wood because it smoked too damn much. *Yes, Pine trees!* You couldn't even use the wood in a fireplace, because it would cake your chimney with creosote. PINE TREES! Ugly, impractical, and spreading like fire all over Alabama.

Yes, they grew all over his state. And others apparently knew it also. One thing had once severely depressed him. He remembered watching television one day and perceiving a comedian joking about the South in general and his beloved Alabama in particular.

"What is always red and ignorant and green and ugly?" asked the fellow. Then he answered himself. "The State of Alabama, because there's nothing down there but rednecks and pine trees!"

It must have been funny to the audience, for they laughed. But it wasn't funny to Clifton. The "redneck" part didn't really bother him. It was the other part, the part about all of the pine trees growing in his state that distressed him. It jabbed him deep down inside with a kind of resigned hopelessness.

It was evident, then, that pine trees actually incited emotional turmoil inside Clifton. And his schizophrenia probably did make it worse. But his uncle, the relative with whom Clifton shared a beat up mobile home, did not think there was anything wrong with his nephew. His Uncle Buck resented Clifton. He didn't care for the fact that he had to share his small pension, as well as his trailer, with a person who was in apparent good physical health, but didn't pull his weight. He considered his nephew as nothing but a parasite—and disliked him intensely. The only reason he permitted Clifton to stay with him was because of the long ago request his sister had made on her offspring's behalf on her deathbed. She had made her brother promise to shelter her disturbed son.

Clifton didn't care much for his benefactor, either. In fact, he detested Uncle Buck every bit as much as Uncle Buck detested him. Yes, he hated the old man—almost as much as he hated pine trees. There were numerous reasons for this, one of them being his uncle's incessant nagging at him to get a job. Another reason had to do with football. In Alabama, where people practically *live* for college football, it's either the University of Alabama Crimson Tide, or the Auburn Tigers. And while the uncle preferred the former, the nephew pulled for the latter. But the main reason Clifton hated his uncle was the fact that Uncle Buck actually *liked* those ugly plant things called pine trees. Every year, at Christmas time, his uncle used young loblolly pines for Christmas trees. He actually preferred them over the traditional cedars, firs or spruces. And this always ruined the holidays for Clifton. After all, whoever heard of a stupid *pine* Christmas tree! Yes, Uncle Buck apparently *loved* pine trees! Years ago, he had actually planted the damn things around the trailer; and now, all grown up, they seemed to press themselves around Clifton. It might have been his schizophrenia, but Clifton felt intimidated by them—almost suffocated by them. And at night, when the wind blew through their branches, Clifton could swear that the pines were talking to him—and not in very amiable ways, either. They seemed to whisper nasty things to him, to mock him, even threaten him. And although it is the somber truth that people suffering the disease, schizophrenia, often hear ghostly voices in their heads, Clifton could swear that it was no audio hallucination. He feared that the pines really were communicating to him evil intentions.

So that was the situation: a resentful old man and his disturbed nephew despising each other—but living together below the poverty level in a rundown trailer somewhere in Alabama and surrounded by pine trees.

* * *

"Why don't you get yourself a job and start payin' for your keep around here?" They were sitting at the breakfast table, and Uncle Buck was nagging Clifton again.

Clifton must have heard this question a million times; and he was sick to death of it. But he was always obliged to justify himself, and he always answered the same way. "I've told you I couldn't hold a job even if I was able to get one. You know that I sometimes have trouble thinking the right way in my mind."

"Trouble thinkin' the right way, hell! Your thinkin's just as good as anybody's. You just think you got a free meal and board ticket around here just 'cause some shrink *told* you you got trouble thinkin' right. Well, let me tell you, if it wasn't for your momma beggin' me to let you stay here when she died, I'd kick your lazy ass right out of here! I'm tired of supportin' you. And no matter how much I loved my sister, I just might kick you out anyways!"

It was at this point that Clifton had always remained silent; for this threat always scared him. But this morning, for some reason, he was feeling bold. He was tired of his uncle always having the last word. He decided that it was finally time to respond to this old threat.

"I'd like to see you try it, old man."

Uncle Buck didn't reply right away. He was a bit stunned. After all, this was the first time his nephew had ever defied him about this. It was the first time that his authority in this situation had been challenged. But he quickly replied to the upstart.

"What was that you said? You'd better apologize to me for that, or I'll get my shotgun and kick you outta here right now—you leech!"

Now things had really taken a nasty turn; for it was the first time his uncle had used this epithet on Clifton. Whirling, angry thoughts began spinning in Clifton's mind. He had never been called a "leech" before, and he didn't like it at all. It just wasn't so. He wasn't a parasite. He was just schizophrenic—the doctor had pronounced him so—and he was simply unable to make his own living. And, anyway, it wasn't as if he enjoyed this situation. He hated it. He was sick of the beat up old trailer, sick of the poverty, and especially sick of the pine trees surrounding him. Yes, the pine trees! His uncle's precious pine trees! The pine trees that whispered taunts and insults to him when the wind blew. He decided it was finally time to take action—time to cut down those damn conifers. But right now it was more important to tend to his human nemesis. Hell, he was disturbed anyway. If they caught him, he could simply plead insanity. The shrinks would back him up. They wouldn't send him to jail.

"You!" Now that Clifton had formed his resolve, he was suddenly a mad dog. All the pent-up rage that had been pressure cooking for years was released. He was shouting in Uncle Buck's face. "You and your old trailer! You and your stupid Crimson Tide! You and your goddamn pine trees! Show you respect? I'll show you my hands around your throat!"

Then Clifton pounced…Clifton squeezed…Clifton giggled like some crazy little kid….

He waited until dusk to dispose of the body. He figured it was safer that way. When it was dark enough, he began digging a hole out in the back yard in the middle of the pine trees. He would bury the body in this hole. Then, first thing in the morning, he would grab his uncle's chain saw and cut down every one of his green enemies.

So that was the plan. "A good plan," thought Clifton, as he worked with the shovel. He just hoped that the storm that was building up in the west would hold off until he finished his task. It was already sprinkling, and Clifton, who was none too fond of thunderstorms, dug faster. No, he didn't care for thunderstorms at all. For thunderstorms meant lightening and high winds and tornados—and these things could kill you.

So Clifton hurried up; and when he was satisfied with the dimensions of the hole, a quite narrow and shallow one, he went to fetch Uncle Buck.

It was now very dark, with the rain now falling heavily and the wind blowing strongly; but Clifton, although apprehensive of the storm, continued on with his task. With the aid of the light of an old kerosene lantern, he dragged the body out of the trailer and through the yard to the hole. Once there, he dumped Uncle Buck into the grave, then quickly covered him with the dirt. Finishing this, and eager to take cover from the storm, he retreated to the trailer.

But just because he made it inside didn't mean his fear of the raging weather outside subsided. He felt a little safer, but the trepidation remained. Meanwhile the storm intensified. It was hailing now, and the wind was like a hurricane. To make matters worse, the storm had knocked out the power, leaving him with only the feeble rays of the light produced by the lantern. And then something else, something even more fearful than the raging weather became manifest. It was the pine trees; they were talking to him again. Not merely talking. Competing with the loud noise of the storm, they seemed to be positively roaring at him.

"You're ours, Clifton! You're ours!" He could swear that he heard them shouting this out. He tensed. He was terrified. He was nauseous with fear.

Then…BANG! The wind blew open the trailer door. He jerked with the sound; then, when he was composed enough, he went to shut the door.

"Owww!" Having discarded his shoes, he now stepped on something. It had been blown in by the wind. It was a pine cone.

"Idiot shit!" he cried through clenched teeth.

"You're ours, Clifton! You're ours!"

And he could feel the vomit pressing up his gullet. He rushed for the bathroom, but didn't make it. It gushed out on the floor. Thoughts of mops, water and cleaners now entered his mind. He went to fetch these articles. He reached for the cleaner. And what kind of cleaner? Pine, *pine*, PINE!

For a time Clifton could only stand there whispering the word "pine" idiotically, or maybe schizophrenically, over and over. But his trance was abruptly ended by a clash of thunder, immediately followed by a crashing sound at the ceiling. The wind had blown a tree limb in through it, and Clifton knew, without looking, what kind of limb it was.

"You're ours, Clifton! You're ours!"

Scared to death, he put his hands to his ears, but he could still hear them. They were calling to him, threatening him. They were brushing up against the trailer all around. They were pressing in on him. And he suddenly realized it was time to get the hell out of there. And so he grabbed the victim's wallet and keys and fled outside to Uncle Buck's old Chevy Belair.

The storm raged all around him, but undeterred, he started the car and, with wheels spinning mud, backed it out of the yard and steered it for the highway. But where could he go? Not east. Georgia, after all, was famous for her pines. Not west. Mississippi had more than her share of them. Not south. There were millions of pine trees in Florida. North! Yes, north, to Tennessee, to the Great Smoky Mountains—where he knew there were hardly any pines at all.

So he headed north. But even though the windows were rolled up, he could still hear the pines along the road now positively bellowing at him.

"YOU'RE OURS, CLIFTON! YOU'RE OURS!"

And in spite of the treacherous conditions, he floored it.

That, however, he should never have done, because around a curve ahead on a bridge was a stalled truck, loaded down with pulpwood—the longest log sticking out behind and tagged with the usual red flag.

Clifton saw the flashing blinkers as he rounded the turn, and he knew that there was no chance of avoiding a collision. He couldn't swerve; on this wet road, he knew he would slide right into the truck. He couldn't brake; he knew he would skid right into it. So he did nothing. His foot remained where it was on the accelerator, but things seemed to slow down, anyway. In slow motion he approached the truck, the log with the flag coming right toward his face. An image of Jayne Mansfield, the star killed near Biloxi in a similar fashion, arose and vanished in his mind. And the last thing to occur to him was the knowledge of the nature of the wood that was going to finish him.

Pine…

The two morticians were standing over the body. They had just finished stitching up around the throat, reattaching the severed head.

"Not much left of his face, is there?" asked one.

"No, there's not," replied the other. "But it won't matter. If anybody comes to visit, we'll just keep the box closed on this one."

"Speaking of the box, what kind will we use for him?"

"Well, this guy had no family. The sheriff said he probably murdered his uncle—who was the only relative he had. And since he had no insurance or any other assets to speak of, we'll go the cheap route. We'll use pine."

PROCEDURE MONOMANIA

One might well have imagined the great shock I experienced when, upon returning to America from an extended stay in Europe, I received the information that my dearest friend had been committed by the state into the care of a mental institution. At first this news was entirely unacceptable to me. Indeed, I refused to believe it at all until an actual visit with him in the asylum confirmed for me the terrible truth.

Although I had always thought of my physician friend, Hylas Mire, as a rather eccentric person, I had never once harbored any doubts as to the stability of his mind. However, when I was allowed to see him, I was greatly saddened to witness the state to which the once bright and knowledgeable doctor had succumbed. Once an intelligent chiropractic physician, journalist, and lecturer, he had obviously become a hopeless lunatic.

In the room where they had him confined, the doctor was standing behind a vacant chair, twisting in his hands some imaginary something that, in his disordered mind, he evidentially supposed was stationed there. Repeatedly he would deliver a hard wrench in space, then shout out in an agonized voice, "It's still not right!" Over and over he did this, completely unaware of my efforts to attract his attention. Even when I seized his hand and attempted to force him to recognize me, he did nothing but violently shake free of my grasp and continue on with his wrenching and shouting. The attendant informed me that he did this continually, day after day, remaining oblivious to anyone or anything other than the chair and his psychotic endeavors with it. I was also told that he would not submit himself willingly to any form of psychotherapy, and that when he was forcibly drawn away from the chair, he would scream so loudly and incessantly that the nurses were always obliged to return him to his station and free him to continue his wrenching.

I watched Dr. Mire's activity with the chair for nearly half an hour, and during this time, in addition to the great sorrow I felt for him, a strong desire arose within me to discover, if possible, any insights from the doctor's journals or lectures which might lead me to an understanding of the nature of my friend's madness.

With this resolve, then, I departed the hospital and became subsequently engaged in the preparation of a journey to Picten University, my friend's alma mater, where I expected to discover the most comprehensive collection of the doctor's literary works.

Upon arriving at the campus, I wasted no time, but immediately read anything I could find that was composed by the doctor. For four days I devoted a great amount of time and energy in research, until I was finally rewarded with one of his compositions, an unpublished manuscript, which I am today certain provides the key to the mystery of Dr. Mire and his chair.

And now, in order to enlighten anyone interested in the nature of my friend's insanity, I present here, with the permission of Picten University, that same manuscript. It is titled *Procedure Monomania: A Study of Mental Turmoil*

Although I am a chiropractor by trade, not a psychiatrist, disturbances within the human mind intrigue me—especially the one that I shall examine in this paper. And I believe that, due to exhaustive research on the particular mental affliction I shall discuss here, I am qualified to write a competent thesis on it. With that noted, let me begin this essay by stating that there are many, far too many, afflictions of the human mind. While it is only proper that the more serious and common of mental illnesses receive the larger proportion of psychiatric research, I contend that there is one particular disease of the mind, probably *more* serious than most others, that has not received proper attention. Ironically, this is because those who suffer this psychosomatic disorder almost always retain enough rationality within them to prevent them from realizing the fact that they are, indeed, disturbed. But the tragic fact of the matter is that "procedure monomania"—as I have termed this illness—is very serious. In its more extreme forms, it can be as devastating as schizophrenia. And although this disease is characterized by frequent and intense anguish, even torment, it hardly ever occurs to the victim that he should seek professional help. Very few of the subjects consult psychiatrists; thus, without the patients from which to extract the related information, this particular illness remains largely a mystery. This is not to imply that the psychiatric profession is *completely* ignorant as to the cause and treatment of this disease. They have attempted to consider this disorder as just an extreme example of "obsessive compulsive disorder." They offer counsel, as well as medication. But these treatments are often ineffective. And besides, the illness I am concerned with is *not* mere OCD. It is much more serious.

It is my intention in this paper to present a detailed study of the nature of this affliction. It is my hope here that, by presenting a report on the basic characteristics of procedure monomania, I shall accomplish two objectives: (1) I shall attract more attention to this malady from the psychiatric institution and thus inspire more research as to its nature and possible remedy; and (2) I shall alert procedure monomaniacs to their affliction and thus convince them to seek help, what little there is of it, from the psychiatric establishment.

Procedure monomania, or P.M., is characterized by intense endeavors to perform usually simple, ordinary actions in perfect accordance with complicated procedures developed by the victim and deemed by him as the "proper" or "correct" ways in which to perform these actions. While unaffected people look upon these actions with nothing more than the normal simplicity which should be accorded them, the procedure monomaniac holds these actions in the light of irrational complexity. P.M. prevents its victim from considering these actions in simple, natural ways; and this handicap causes him to believe that, at least when he is concerned, there are *absolutely correct* ways to accomplish the actions. These same actions he must perform in *perfect accordance* with how he has determined is *perfectly correct*; and it is during his usually several attempts to accomplish a "perfect procedure" wherein his anguish is manifested. The longer he tries, the more difficult his objective usually becomes. But he *must* persevere until a "perfect procedure" satisfies his monomania. There is no alternative, no compromise; he must obtain "perfection." Otherwise, he would suffer an unendurable feeling of unachieved "technical perfection." And the really ironic aspect about this disorder is that the actual reason for performing the act condescends to insignificance! The *ends* become nothing to the procedure monomaniac; it is the *means* that become paramount.

Now I shall illustrate this affliction with possible procedures to which P.M. can subject its victims, so the reader will understand how really serious and tragic this illness actually is.

A procedure monomaniac washes his hands in preparation to eat a meal. But as he is drying them, he happens to notice a small speck of dirt under one of his fingernails that he failed to remove. To the procedure monomaniac, this is absolutely intolerable. His hands must be *thoroughly* clean, and this represents the beginning of his difficulties.

Now, most people, if they even cared, would probably remedy this minor detail by applying a toothpick, or some other such tool, to the nail in question and, upon removing the speck of dirt, leave it at that. Not so with the procedure monomaniac. Within his psychosomatic mind, he concludes that, because he did not devote enough attention to this particular nail when he washed his hands, his action of hand washing is "incorrect." It was not "perfectly accomplished." He would not be content to simply remove the speck from the nail. No, he must repeat the entire hand washing action—and during the procedure, clean not only the dirty nail, but all of his nails whether they need cleaning or not. He is *compelled* to wash his hands again, for his affliction reigns supreme. It actually coerces him to repeat the process. For if he did not obey its dictates, P.M. would cause him intolerable misery. Am I understood here? He would actually feel something very close to *guilt*! Yes, guilt—rampaging throughout his mind. He would feel too anguished to sit down to eat his dinner unless he had washed his hands in the "perfectly correct" manner.

And so, just as thoroughly as he did a short while ago, he washes his hands again—this time paying great attention to his fingernails. But it turns out that he was too careful with his nails; for as he starts to dry his hands, he realizes, with a strong tinge of frustration, that, although he did manage to lather and rinse his hands "correctly," he forgot to retrieve, beforehand, a clean, fresh towel with which to dry them. Now, this business about the fresh towel was already a regular part of his hand washing action, but due to too much preoccupation in the cleaning of his fingernails, it completely slipped his mind to secure in advance for himself the necessary clean article of laundry. This oversight "ruins" the second attempt, and the only alternative is to try the whole thing again—only, of course, after procuring another clean towel. This he does with great care and precaution. After all, he must not "contaminate" the clean towel with too much direct contact from his still "dirty" hands.

When he is prepared for the third attempt, he, with increasing anxiety, washes his hands again. He finishes, and, with great relief, starts to leave the bathroom. But just as he touches the doorknob, he remembers with much torment and self-reproach that he had forgotten to sing the little children's ditty, "This is the Way We Wash Our Hands." Now, obviously, singing this silly little song while washing the hands can contribute absolutely nothing of sanitary value to the action—and our neurotic friend is well aware of this. He also feels foolish and ridiculous singing it. Nevertheless, as he had decided a while back before this particular hand-washing ordeal, the subject of this song is so *exactly* associated with what he is now attempting to accomplish, that the singing of the tune is only a "proper" addition to the process. It is just as integral as anything else in "perfectly" washing the hands—thus it *must* be sung. He had sung the ditty during the first two attempts, but the episode with the towel had disturbed him enough for him to completely overlook it during the third attempt.

It follows, then, that, upon procuring yet another clean towel, he washes his hands for the fourth time. Having almost completed this attempt—with everything so far perfectly correct—he nervously prepares to "consummate" the act by swallowing one drink of water from the faucet. Whether or not he is actually thirsty is immaterial, for he has already determined that this is only the "proper" way to conclude the procedure. Upon swallowing, the sensation of the descending water seems a little too perceptible. And this, to his great agony, can only mean that the volume of water he consumed was too far above his "correct" average. He concludes that he had practically *gulped* his water; and because a gulp suggests a rather greedy nature about it, it puts a sour, intolerable aspect on the concluding act of the hand washing action. Thus the fourth attempt is just as "imperfect" as the previous ones. By now he feels like screaming, but the excruciating void manifested by not attaining "perfection" leaves him no choice but to continue washing his hands.

During the next try, he gets too much lather on his wrists. And because he is supposed to be washing his *hands*—not his *wrists*—he stops right there and starts over. It would be pointless to continue on with the fifth attempt, for it has already been "ruined."

Almost immediately after he begins the sixth attempt, he screams and pounds his forehead. He has forgotten the towel again.

Over and over the neurotic man washes his hands—his concentration becoming more intense, his exertions more strenuous. Consider the vast extent that this irrationality has superseded the actual reason for washing the hands. Our disturbed friend most certainly has to be aware that his hands were clean enough an hour or so ago, but that has become completely irrelevant to him. Instead, sink, soap and water have degenerated into actual means of torture.

The individual washes his hands again and again until he finally achieves an action that he finally interprets as being "perfectly correct." And it is only a matter of interpretation after all, simply because there exists no such achievement as "perfectly" washing the hands—or for that matter, "perfectly" doing anything. But, nevertheless, he feels that he has at last "qualified" himself for his dinner. He emerges from the towel cluttered bathroom with raw, red hands to consume the now icy food that has, by this time, actually become less sanitary than the hands with which he has so laboriously and torturously prepared to handle it!

Now please consider: I have just explained how such an ordinarily simple action as the washing of hands can become a terrible, complicated ordeal to some people—a mountainous obstacle that the affected person must regularly surmount. *Think of it!* I am discussing an illness that can cause its victims to hold the otherwise harmless act of hand washing in absolute dread!

But the washing of hands is just one example. P.M. can complicate any action that should otherwise be simple. It can affect such activities as walking up or down stairs, opening or closing doors, eating, reading or getting in and out of bed.

Nothing humans do may be considered to be outside the influence of procedure monomania. This can even include the act of copulation. One might imagine the difficulties arising from the *must* for "perfectly correct" sexual intercourse. It could be complicated and agonizing enough if only one of the parties suffered from P.M., but consider the possible chaos if both partners were procedure monomaniacs:

Very quickly following penetration, the male makes what he decides is a, call it, "technical mistake." However much he hates it, he must immediately repress his drive and withdraw. His P.M. is all powerful—even stronger than testosterone—and its dictates *must* be obeyed. The ominous knowledge that, had he continued, the completed act would be "imperfect," renders any continuation towards sexual climax intolerable, even impossible. And so, following a miserable ten or fifteen minutes—or the passage of enough time for them to consider themselves as starting relatively afresh—they initiate the second attempt. This time, however, the female does something "wrong," or "incorrect." Thus now *she* demands an immediate cessation. Following another interval they attempt it for the third time. But this time they both become tangled up in procedure monomanic "imperfection," and they literally scream in agonized frustration.

Thus, P.M. can infect man's most pleasurable experience, turning it into a complex, excruciating ordeal. *Think of it!* I am discussing a malady that can turn an otherwise beautiful, pleasurable pastime into a dreadful, insufferable nightmare!

I have expounded but a few of the infinite ways in which procedure monomania can turn life into an unbearable existence. P.M. can affect any action; and I believe that the last example I have portrayed especially illustrates how serious is the need for more research regarding this affliction.

In concluding, I must state that I have no doubts that what I have discussed in this paper will be taken by many as being highly exaggerated, if not completely fictitious, but this, I am distressed to point out, is only to be expected when most, if not all, mental disturbances are presented in the style, utilized here, of closely detailed exemplification. However, I have still accomplished my purpose here if I have successfully illustrated to any sufferer of P.M. the pure nonsense—even the complete silliness—of believing that certain actions must be performed in these "perfect" manners. It is my express and genuine hope that I, through this study, might help the sufferer to either cease these activities on his own, or, if unable to do so, convince him to seek psychiatric help with this terrible affliction.

Upon relating the information contained in the preceding study to the events surrounding my friend's commitment into an asylum, I understood at once the mystery of the doctor and his chair. And now, to enlighten anyone interested in the case, let me record how it happened that my friend was put away.

Dr. Mire, you recall, was a chiropractor. It so happened that, during a session between the doctor and one of his patients, a female, the doctor's receptionist, who was busily engaged at her desk, was suddenly startled by the sound of several piercing shrieks from within Dr. Mire's treatment room. These initial screams were soon joined by a loud masculine voice shouting, "*It's still not right*!" over and over. And this caused the receptionist, thinking it best that she check into this matter, to enter the mentioned room.

Dr. Mire, as it turned out, was apparently a procedure monomaniac, himself, and it seems that his report on the illness was written as much for his own benefit as for the benefit of his fellow sufferers. But it seems that, after having failed to persuade himself to try to stop submitting to the illness's dictates and seek help, his procedure monomania had finally invaded his occupation itself.

When the receptionist opened the door of the treatment room, she beheld the chiropractor standing behind his seated patient applying his professional skills towards alleviating a cramp in her neck. But the shouting Dr. Mire, his face sweating profusely and horribly contorted, was in a very agonized condition. His condition, however, was not quite as unenviable as that of the woman in the chair. By the time the receptionist opened the door, the patient had stopped screaming. She was obviously dead; her neck was broken. But Dr. Mire, now apparently insane, was still violently wrenching and twisting the head. It is supposed that he was trying to eliminate the neck cramp in the "perfectly correct" manner,

Author's note: Evidently, Dr. Mire finally did attain what he interpreted as a "perfect procedure," for it happened that he eventually ceased his agonized activity with the chair. And although he shall probably be confined for the rest of his life in the sanitarium, he, having consented to medication and council, is, as I write this, doing much better.

THE WOMB AND THE WINDOW

Pregnant women disturbed Eddie. Ever since he could remember this had been so. Upon seeing one of these people—especially one greatly advanced—a potent and terrible feeling of envy would immediately surge up from deep within him and seize his whole being. He couldn't resist it. It was black and agonizing, yet almost erotic. It fastened his eyes on the bulge like immovable lasers. *Envy!* Envy of the warmth, envy of the protection enjoyed by the wee body he knew was inside. *Envy!* Envy that flooded through him out of control. He just couldn't handle it, couldn't accept it. He just couldn't stand the actuality of babies inside of wombs—tiny people inside such heavenly places.

It was a tortuous, insufferable ordeal that happened to him every time he saw a mother-to-be; and if she remained in his presence for too long a time, Eddie, absolutely helpless in the vise of the terrible trance-like fascination the bulge produced upon him, would find himself in even more difficulty. He would feel the blood rushing down below from some sort of haywire, anything but pleasant, sexual excitement. He would also start to tremble out of control. And then the worst thing, the most fearful thing of all, would begin to happen. He would feel his very sanity being threatened by the strong hint of a nameless growing madness. Maybe it was something like schizophrenia. Whatever it was, it seemed to whirl around and around somewhere in his mind; and Eddie feared that this powerful, spinning suggestion of insanity might one day, if given the chance, suck in his ability to think soundly and spin it into chaos.

But if Eddie had all this going against him, he still had, at least, one good thing in his life. And that was his pretty girlfriend, Jane. Or at least that was how he chose to think of her. She lived in the upstairs apartment of a secluded old house in the country—the same house in which he himself resided downstairs.

Yeah, she was his girlfriend all right. Of course she was! Oh, it was true that they didn't sleep together. Nor did they kiss or even hold hands; but they did do other things with each other. They would often eat lunch, play cards and watch television together. And sometimes they would even go out on what Eddie, at least, considered as "dates" to the movies. So didn't these activities they shared, however platonic, qualify her as his girl? In Eddie's desperate mind they certainly did; and he loved her…madly.

And because he loved her so madly, she was always the subject he chose to masturbate about. Whenever he felt the need, he would retreat to the bathroom and lose himself in sexual fantasy.

It would all begin normally enough. He would picture Jane, unclad and beautiful, lying on a bed. But quickly it would get strange. For then he would imagine himself shrinking. He would become smaller and smaller until, when curled up, he would be about the size of a basketball. Then he would imagine himself swimming through the air towards Jane's middle. And it was when he met the waist, but kept on swimming in with a delicious feathery-like resistance, that the sugary feelings generated by his busy hand would start radiating through his body in earnest. Once inside her, he would curl up tightly into the fetal position, pressing the soft interior of the womb outward. And now he would come to the best part of all. And this was imagining a small peephole opening up in front of his face, allowing him to see the outside. And it was here that Eddie's toes were ready to curl and his sugar about to shoot, for he had come to the best part of all. And this was imagining himself peeking out through this tiny little hole at monsters: ugly, scary and evil monsters. It was sort of like the feeling of peeking out at horror movies through the safety screen of one's fingers. Or like camping out and peeking at imaginary, scary creatures in trees and bushes from the warmth and protection of a sleeping bag. It was all of that and more. It was the final ingredient—the royal jelly itself. They were scary, they were ugly, they were evil monsters. But they couldn't get him because he was *inside*, and they were *outside*. He could peek out at them and giggle. It was ecstasy. It was ejaculation.

Eddie indulged himself in this way quite frequently; and it never occurred to him how strange it would appear to someone else. But it was even more ironic in that the idea that turned him on also seemed to be the same thing that caused him such distress: a bulging feminine waist. Some sort of impossible paradox seemed to be involved. There was, however, an explanation. The envy, the hell arose from being *outside* the bulge and having to look at it, and the pleasantness arose from the imagination of being *inside* the bulge and looking out of it.

Yes, this fantasy was very strange all right, but Eddie was too much in love with Jane to worry about anything being seriously wrong with him. Too much in love to worry about mental problems and sexual deviations. And why, he happened to wonder one day, shouldn't he *tell* her he loved her? He already considered her his girlfriend, but how much nicer it would be if she could become the kind of girlfriend that he could actually hold and kiss! It certainly would be a lot more fun. And wouldn't it clear the way for this kissing and other good stuff if he simply opened up to her? Of course it would! (Eddie was irrationally sure of himself in this respect.) And once she replied that she loved him also—and he had no doubt that she would—he would be free to draw his face up to hers, like in the movies, and kiss her mouth. And then they would get in bed together where Eddie could curl up and embrace her middle as tightly as he could.

"Jane, you and I have been seeing each other for a long time, haven't we?" They were eating lunch together, and Eddie, fortified with a couple of beers, was ready to tell Jane that he loved her.

"Yeah, I suppose we have, Eddie."

"Well, lately, I've been thinking about something pretty important about us. Jane, there's something I need to tell you." Eddie could feel something rushing in his head.

"Yes…what is it?" Jane seemed a little ill at ease.

"I love you, Jane!" Eddie didn't waste any time. And he was practically shouting. "I need to get close to you. I need to get close to your...body." He had started to say "abdomen," but he didn't because he thought that that might have seemed silly to her.

Jane did not respond for some time. She seemed a bit stunned. But finally she spoke. "Eddie, I didn't mean for you to get the wrong idea about our relationship. I'm satisfied with just being friends with you. Besides, I think you should know that I've met someone else. I meant to tell you this earlier. It was pretty much a whirlwind thing; and I'm already in love with him. His name is Eric, and he's simply wonderful. He's young and handsome—and smart, too. He made a million off of real estate before he was twenty. And soon we're leaving the States to live in Europe. I've already made arrangements to leave here. Next month, Eddie, I'll be living in my own castle in England!"

And that was it—poison. First the words penetrated and registered; then Eddie felt himself caving in. Like acid, her words seemed to burn his soul away. She wasn't his girlfriend, and never would be. For a moment an idea that he was a demon's plaything seemed very credible to him. And when recalled the once bright, but now dissolved hopes he had had about this evening, something inside him saw a cruel joke about it and laughed in spite of the pain.

What would you do if you were poor, strange Eddie? With the one you love an ocean away and with someone else, how do you suppose you would pass the long painful time? What would your average day be like?

Well, the first thing you do after waking up in the morning is think about her. You think about faraway Jane. Then you take a shower, cook and eat your breakfast and think some more about faraway Jane. Then you drive to the textile plant where you work, and still you think about the one you love. Finally, after work is finished and you are home again, you pull it out and *really* think about her.

Yes, there she is, all naked and beautiful... Now shrink yourself. Get smaller and smaller... There! You're now the perfect size. Now start swimming to her...yes, right towards her middle... There! Can you feel it? Can you feel the feathery, delicious resistance of her flesh as you swim on in? Do you feel the sugar beginning to work up? Oh, *man*! You're inside her womb now. You're inside paradise! Now curl up in a ball...slowly...slowly. Can you feel the soft warm tightness around you? Can you imagine the wonderful bulge you're creating? Now get ready...there's the peephole! Look! Do you see them? Look how ugly and scary they are! But they can't get you. You don't have to worry about that because you're *inside* and they are *outside*. You peek out at them through your tiny little window and giggle. It's sugar and honey! It's jelly and jam! It's—

"Jane!" you scream out her name as you ejaculate...

But the ecstasy is very fleeting. It's gone in a flash; and now you start thinking about the way things actually are. You think about Jane being with that rich guy somewhere across the ocean thousands of miles away; and as a result you suffer strong depression. So what should you do about it? Get something to eat? Watch television? Work up another one? Why not?

And so you do it again, but it's not as good as the first one. It takes a lot longer, and when it is over, you feel drained, even exhausted. It also leaves you more despondent than ever because you know it hasn't changed a thing about Jane and that rich guy. You know that they are still together—maybe even married by now. You could beat off forever, but it wouldn't help you. And so, trying to resign yourself to this painful reality, you get up from the commode and prepare to continue living your lonely life. After supper you watch T.V. until you decide it's time to retire for the night. And it is when you're lying in bed in the darkness that you pray to God that you don't have the nightmare again.

But you have it anyway. First, you find yourself standing naked in the middle of a dismal nowhere. One moment you're alone; the next moment you're not alone. It's Jane! But you feel ashamed because you're naked. You seem to be cold also, and scared of some unknown something. So you ask her to let you inside—to let you crawl into her womb. But she says nothing. She is like a statue. In desperation you clasp her ankles and whimper. But she says nothing. She is like a statue.

Then you do hear something. It's not Jane's voice, but it is very close by. You look up toward the sound. You recoil violently. For Jane is no longer slim. She bulges! She has become one of *them*!

Now! Can you feel it? Can you feel the envy? It's virulent, hellish, overwhelming. Can you feel the flooding excitement, the unpleasant rush down below? And now! The most terrible, dreadful thing of all. It's that unknown whirling something. That spinning suggestion of madness that threatens to suck down your whole mind and sling it around and around until sanity is no more.

But listen! You hear that voice again. It's coming out of Jane's body. It sounds like giggling—smothered giggling. Yes, something is giggling, but at what? Then you suddenly know. It's giggling at *you*! Because it can suddenly see you through a—

Wheeeeee! Around and around and around it goes. Around and around and—

You wake up screaming—your shaking body drenching the bed with sweat and piss.

A year had passed since Jane moved away. Then, a simple postcard he received one day in the mail seemed to promise Eddie a reprieve from his miserable existence. On one side was a picture of Big Ben; on the other side was the following script:

> *Dear Eddie,*
>
> *Sorry to have taken so long to write. Am coming home to my old apartment above you. Already arranged it with our landlady. I broke up with Eric. What a jerk! I've got more great news for you too, but I'll wait and surprise you with it. Be home the first of next month,*
>
> *Love, Jane*

Eddie found it hard to believe what he had read. It had been so long since anything really good had happened in his life that he wondered if he were dreaming. He read the message several times and fondled the postcard repeatedly. Yes, it was real; and he was definitely awake. And with this realization, something inside him cartwheeled with joy. An angel must have finally chased away the demons from his life. Jane was coming home! She was coming back to *him*! She finally *did* want to be his girlfriend after all! She had said something about a surprise for him, but he already knew what it was. The surprise was that she had finally fallen in love with him and wanted to let him know! Had she not hinted as much in the final two words of farewell in her message? Yes, Jane *loved* him; and she would be home on the first day of next month to tell him that!

Eddie was not merely engaged in wishful thinking here. He truly believed he knew how Jane would react when she saw him again. Maybe he was just too desperate for love. He was certainly irrational, probably even schizophrenic.

It was the first of the month. It was Friday. It was here; and Eddie hardly knew what to do with himself. To say that he was excited would be quite the understatement; all day at work he was hard down below. And when the textile plant finally closed for the day, he drove home very quickly through the gathering dusk. And when he turned in the driveway and, for the first time in a year, perceived lights on upstairs, he almost swooned.

But he didn't hesitate. He got out of the car and ran up the outside stairs to her door. Arriving there, he knocked, waited a few moments, then knocked again.

No answer. Where was Jane?

Eddie quickly grew impatient. He tried the doorknob, found that it turned freely, and decided to walk on in. Once inside, he called out the name of his true love.

No answer? Where was Jane?

He kept wondering about this as he slowly moved through the apartment. Eventually he found himself outside the bedroom. Hoping he could discover her in here, he gently rapped on the door and called out her name once more.

No answer! Where was Jane!

Eddie had come too far to turn away now. He slowly turned the knob and opened the door. Perceiving darkness inside, he ran his hand along the wall, feeling for the light switch. He found it. He clicked it.

And there was Jane. Yes, Jane—home at last! She was lying on the bed sleeping—probably worn out from her flight home.

But he wasn't about to leave and wait for later. He had to wake up his girlfriend right now and hear her say that she loved him. And so he crept closer.

It was a warm night, and Jane had not covered herself with the bedclothes. And she was clad only in a bra and panties. She was lying on her side, her back to him. And this was why he didn't see it until he had reached her bedside.

Jane...bulged...

Jane bulged! And Eddie could do nothing but stand there and stare. He tried to disbelieve what he was seeing, but the evidence mercilessly remained. Oh, God, no! Jane bulged! *This*, then was the news she had mentioned in the postcard. *This* was the big surprise.

Nightmare come true! Two lasers for eyes, unmoving, unblinking, searing against the dreadful largeness. The envy—vile, poisonous, insufferable. The uncontrollable trembling. The blood rushing down below. The familiar threat of an ultimate madness arising and spinning and attacking his sanity. But this time everything was horribly worse, horribly intensified. Because this time the pregnant girl was Jane! And everything was hell to the tenth power!

Eddie, his mind and body in the midst of all this distress, was now, suddenly and somehow, aware of one thing. He knew he had to get out of there right then. He realized that if he did not, he would finally be overwhelmed by that nameless spinning something and be lost forever. He knew that this was the showdown of his life. It was either retreat and salvage what sanity remained in his mind, or stay there and completely lose it.

But he couldn't just turn and walk away from this scene. There seemed to be no way in the world he could. Like a black hole, the bulge pulled his eyes into it, steadily aggravating all the bad things that were going on with him.

But he finally managed to put himself in motion. He found it possible, however, to only move backwards—and only very slowly. He managed one rearward step; and as he did so, he felt that horrible vortex suck even stronger at his mind. But he resisted it as best he could; for if he didn't, he knew it meant disaster. He took another step backwards, and again fought to hang on. Then he managed another…and another. But now his teeth were chattering; he was racked by violent spasms. The very need for logic and reason was beginning to seem ludicrous. And sanity itself, a fleeting, nebulous conception. But he somehow persevered and continued his retreat. Four more tottering, rearward steps were accomplished…and he felt his groping hand finally brush against the edge of the door. Now, just one more step backwards, and he could shut the door in front of the terrible scene before him.

But just before he could take that final step, just before he could close the door, something happened on the bed. Actually it was a very trivial thing. Jane, somehow still oblivious to everything, had simply turned over in his direction. But it caused Eddie to notice something about her that he had not noticed before. For a few moments it seemed to be completely natural and harmless. But then it suddenly looked like something else. A something else that was not so natural and harmless. A something else that seemed to form the very basis of his nightmare, his sex drive, his very psyche itself. In schizophrenic fascination Eddie continued to stare at this something else. It caused him to forget everything else—including how desperately he needed to get out of this room. And it was when he realized that it looked *just like* this mentioned something else that the spinning madness finally triumphed, finally sucked him down forever. For it was just too much insult, too much injury, too much hell for him to handle anymore. It just looked too much like a—

Wheeeeee! Around and around and around it goes! Around and around and—

This little hole in Jane's taut belly...this little hole. The unenlightened called it a navel, but he knew better. It was a peephole! What *else* could it be? And it was being utilized. Somebody was peeking out through it, peeking out at him! Who was it? Wait! He knew. It was that rich guy! Who *else* could it be? That rich bastard was in there peeking out. But he was doing more than that. He was making Eddie, the witness of all this, an ugly monster—and feeling all safe and happy with the warm protection of Jane's womb around him. He was so happy that he was giggling. Eddie could plainly hear it echoing in his mind. He was in Jane! Peeking out! Imagining Eddie was a monster! Beating off in there! Not fair! Supposed to be the other way around! It *would* be, god damn it! It *would* be the other way around!

Eddie had no trouble at all in turning away from the bulge now. He had to leave to go find something, but he was coming right back. After all, if he was an evil monster, he might as well act like one.

The next morning the landlady, Miss Bixley, came over to welcome Jane home. Because Miss Bixley was not in the habit of knocking on the doors of people who paid rent to her, she walked right on in. Perceiving no one around, she called out, "Yoo-hoo, anybody home?" She received no answer, but this did not deter her. She would just go see if Jane was sleeping. She started out towards the bedroom, but hadn't gone far before she was arrested by a noise close by. It sounded like giggling—smothered giggling. She listened to it for a few moments, and then found herself a bit hesitant to move any closer to the noise. It sounded too weird—even unwholesome. But Miss Bixley did not retreat. After all, this was her building and it was probably best that she investigate this. With this resolve, then, she continued on closer to the muffled laughter. Arriving outside the closed door of the bedroom she halted. For again the giggles unnerved her. For a few seconds she again hesitated, now feeling a strong urge to actually flee the premises. But she stayed where she was and knocked hard on the door. She, however, received no answer, nor did she interrupt the gigging emanating from within. Again she pounded, and now called out;

but still the giggling continued. Miss Bixley then realized that she must either obey the now overwhelming impulse to get out of that place immediately, or throw open that door right now. And it was her great misfortune to choose the latter…

For the rest of her life, Miss Bixley would harbor a memory of a terrible room. Just beneath the bed on the floor of this room was a red-stained carving knife. Positioned on the red-soaked bed were three naked individuals. Two of them were dead. One of them, a woman, was propped up in a sitting position, her back resting against the headboard. Her head was tilted back over the top of the board and her arms hung limply by her sides. Lying between this woman's legs, his own legs bent together with knees pointing to the ceiling, was a male. His face wasn't visible, but his sex was readily obvious by the part inside his jerking hand. His face was not visible because his whole head was inside where the woman had been ripped open. This was why his voice was smothered. His head was inside where something else used to be, but was torn out. He was giggling and peeking out through the slashed flesh at the third person, another male—but tiny and not quite fully developed—who was lying at the foot of the bed. This third person was supposedly an evil, scary monster.

SHE OF THE OTHER KINGDOM

> *"You have but to truly desire me in your heart; and when that member—just as the comb drips honey—overflows with purity, then I shall have you, in one form or the other..."*
>
> —words for those who seek LOVE

Timothy Seeks was one of those young men who might be called idealistic. He believed in Love. He was in love with Love. He believed that Love in human form existed, and that he was destined to meet Her. He was even convinced that he knew who Love was. Love's name was Toni, Toni Nevare; and ten years ago, he had attended high school with Her. He had never touched or talked to Her, but because Love was magical, he knew She was aware of him. He knew She loved him. After all, Love knows everything, and She is there for whomever looks for Her.

Yes, Timothy was certainly idealistic. So idealistic, in fact, that many people would have considered him as having lost touch with reality.

Timothy loved to look at Toni's picture in his old high school yearbook. She had been chosen most beautiful—no surprise—and it was the portrait of Her accorded this honor that he studied Her face. Love's face, was pleasingly oval with perfectly placed cheekbones; and it was nicely surrounded by thick, flowing shoulder length brown tresses arranged in an unusual but charming style which seemed to hint of a combination of the Hellenic with the antebellum. Below the forehead were pleasing eyebrows arching over enormous blue eyes. Down from the pretty, statuesque nose were full, shapely lips forming a delicious smile. She was clothed in an old-fashioned granny dress—as was the popular style for young women in '71—and was holding in Her lap a rag doll.

And She was posed very well. With face fully toward the camera and body in profile, She reposed on the ground, Her back resting against the trunk of a sycamore tree.

Timothy's favorite place to enjoy the picture was under the shade of an enormous mimosa tree growing in his back yard just outside his bedroom. There were many trees of many kinds growing on the land his father had left him, but his favorite was this mimosa. It had always been his favorite, but he had never really known exactly why. Maybe it was because it was the only member of its species on the land—a circumstance he considered unusual. After all, mimosas were supposed to be among the most prolific of trees. Or maybe it was because of its unusual, even phenomenal size. He knew that mimosas were ordinarily small, quite delicate looking trees, but this particular one was quite large—its limbs spreading out to wondrous lengths. Or maybe it was because it was such an excellent shade tree under which to lie on the grass during the warm, lazy southern afternoons, its low hanging limbs forming a cool, pleasant curtain all around. Or maybe it was because it was so delightful to his eyes—especially on early sunlit spring mornings and late afternoons; for then it appeared as a vast, lavish, golden-bathed bouquet of pretty little green leaves and delicate pink blossoms. But it was *probably* his favorite because of something about the pleasing way it smelled, or something about the graceful way it swayed, or something about the soft way it whispered, when it was embraced by gentle breezes, that always seemed to lead his mind into pleasant fairy tale realms.

Yes, he loved this tree. Almost as much as he loved Love.

When Timothy received his invitation to the ten-year reunion of his high school class, it felt as though his heart would leap out of his body. He rejoiced because he realized that this gathering was to be nothing less than the setting in which he would finally rendezvous with his soul mate, Toni. The time had arrived. There would be no more of his waiting for Love to come to his house and carry him away—as he was wont to fantasize about. He was to meet Her halfway—at their old school. They would come together at the reunion of the Class of '71, then fly away up in the sky somewhere to paradise to live in love forever afterwards.

Yes, again let it be stated that Timothy was a very idealistic young man. Or maybe he was just crazy. Most people would have certainly thought the latter was true.

Never before had Love seemed so beautiful, thought Timothy. It was the night before the reunion, and he was lying in bed gazing, as usual, at Toni's picture. Never before had She seemed so perfectly lovely, and that was probably why he was concentrating this night on the image more deeply than he had ever done so before. Never had he so strongly, so desperately fantasized himself as the rag doll which She held in Her lap. Deeper and deeper he projected himself into the picture until, for the first time ever, he achieved a suspension of disbelief. It suddenly seemed that he actually *was* in the picture. Yes, and that he really *was* the doll—Raggedy Andy—in Her lap. And then, could it just be his fancy or was he really smelling a heavenly feminine perfume? And was it just his fancy or was he really hearing a soft feminine voice sounding—in a long, lingering, caressing whisper—his name? And as he heard, or imagined he heard, his name being called, a strange sweetness within him began to manifest. It seemed to be a tingling, feathery feeling somewhere about his heart. It felt like something loved him, desired him. It soon became so strong that it seemed as if it would lift him away. For an instant, Timothy did not know where he was, who he was, or even *if* he was. It was grand, it was wonderful. It seemed to be, perhaps, just a tiny little bit terrifying too, but somehow in a delicious way.

But then something startled him, immediately bringing him back from wherever he had been. It was a noise, a brushing sound at his window. With Toni in his mind, he quickly turned toward the noise hoping, with a flush of rapture, that, unwilling to wait for the class reunion, She had finally come for him. He hoped to see Her lovely, smiling face outside the window.

But it was not Toni. It was only a branch of the mimosa tree brushing against the window pane.

First, Timothy was bitterly disappointed. His heart felt like it weighed a ton. Then, he grew angry, angry at the mimosa. He felt as if it had fooled him. And if it was ridiculous, even insane to be mad at a tree for simply reacting to the wind, he didn't care. He became so furious, in fact, that he reached toward the window and slammed it down violently to shut off the scent of mimosa blossom—which, tonight, had completely saturated the whole room. Then, lying back down, he turned off the lamp by his bed and, pretending that his pillow was Toni's soft lap, attempted to console himself with reveries of *really* seeing the Special One the next day at the reunion.

Saturday! Saturday! Wonderful, glorious Saturday! It was here. The most important day of his life had finally arrived! Tonight he would finally be forever joined with the sweetest One, the most beautiful One of all. It would be both a conclusion and a commencement. It would represent the end of a lonely, largely depressing existence and the grand beginning of a wholesome, happy life in heaven. Beginning tonight and lasting forever afterwards, he would be united with the actual possessor of that perfect face in the picture. He would be with Love Itself.

Yes, it was finally here, and he had only to contend with the few hours remaining until eight o'clock, the time he had determined as his departure. But, of course, these hours barely crawled by. To Timothy, time seemed immobile. But time is, in fact, very mobile. It passes, and eight o'clock did, indeed, arrive as promptly as it should have. When the hands of the clock had designated that hour, Timothy, dressed in a gray suit with black tie, left the house, jumped in his old Fairlane and started out down the twilit road on his journey to destiny.

But it was rather strange how long the mimosa tree remained framed within the rearview mirror. It became smaller and smaller in the glass, but seemed to just linger and linger there—as if it were reluctant to leave his vision. But it finally disappeared from his sight when he rounded a curve.

It was remarkable that Timothy, notwithstanding his occasional trips into town, had not visited the neighborhood of his old abandoned high school since his long-ago graduation night. And now, as he slowly drove the Fairlane through the crowded parking area adjoining the football field, he realized that the passage of ten years had evidently witnessed little, if any, change in the appearance of his school. But he was not at all interested in the effects of time upon his alma mater. Nor did he care about the changes the first decade of adulthood had wrought upon the Class of '71. Indeed, the effect of time, which had had everything to do with why this assemblage had been organized in the first place, did not absorb him in the least. He couldn't care less about anything concerning this reunion other than that it was to be the setting where he was to be united with the Special One.

He soon found and pulled into a parking place; then he left the car and joined the steady stream of the young men and women heading up the concrete pathway to the gymnasium. For it was that building the organizers of this assemblage had rented and prepared for this event.

As he walked along the pathway toward the gym, Timothy, much relieved that he had so far escaped being recognized, wrung by the hand, slapped on the back and trapped into forced conversation with any former schoolmate, was now immersed in speculation as to how the forthcoming union with Toni would transpire. Was She already inside awaiting his arrival? Or could it be that She would make Her appearance later on? And as he approached the gymnasium—and perceived through its open doorway how brilliantly lit and crowded and noisy it was inside—he found himself wondering why this anything but private and quiet atmosphere had been chosen by Love as the setting for the rendezvous. It seemed to him that this most wonderful event of his life should be consummated in more subtle surroundings. But hesitate, he did not. After all, Love had chosen this place. She had Her own reasons for choosing it for their union; thus he resolved to neither pause nor question.

With the doorway now just two or three steps away, he lowered his face and quickened his stride. He was determined to slip unnoticed through the crowd as quickly as possible and find the most inconspicuous place in the building. Stepping inside, he veered to the left around a group of people standing just inside the doorway and was soon engulfed in the large gathering of the alumni beyond the entrance. Bowing his head and concealing his face as best he could by rubbing his eyes, stroking his brow, and feigning other such hopefully inconspicuous hand to face motions, Timothy hoped he could make it to the rear without being recognized. He was not here to socialize; he was not here to reminisce. He was here *only* to meet Love. As he angled and maneuvered his way deeper into the midst of the chattering, laughing people, he again found himself wondering why this particular location had been chosen as the setting for the great unification. Hot, bright and noisy, this place had all of the ingredients of a depressing dream. The blurred hum of the voices vibrated discordantly in his ears, the heat from all of the bodies was oppressive, and the hateful, all-pervading illumination overruled even the slightest hint of shadow. Above all was the painful dread of being suddenly seized by somebody he used to know and forced into apathetic conversation. The fear of being recognized prevented him from looking into any one of the myriad of faces. But in spite of all these distressing aspects, he pressed on. For he still had faith—and still believed with all of his heart in that which he wanted to, needed to, believe. Namely, that Love would meet him here.

It was with no small relief that Timothy finally reached the largely unoccupied lines of benches adjoining the rear of the building. He seated himself here, and then, bending his body forward and pretending to look at a discarded program of the reunion he found on the floor, he began to steal glances at his surroundings. To his right were the banquet tables, upon which was an extensive buffet. On the opposite side, to the left, he saw the stage platform upon which the rock and roll band was preparing to entertain the participants. Above the bandstand on the wall he read a large white banner with red letters proclaiming, "WELCOME CLASS OF '71." From there his eyes traveled upward—but instantly jerked down and away from the glaring lights above. His gaze landed on the milling, chatting and laughing people congregated on the basketball court. For the first time, the crowd began to interest him. This was not based on any finally surfacing sentimentality. The familiar faces he began to notice did not excite within him even the smallest desire to mingle and become reacquainted with his old schoolmates. It was just that he started to wonder why these people were having such a good time here. *So what* if it had been ten years since graduation? So what if it had been twenty or fifty or a hundred years! What value was a high school reunion—what value was anything—unless it formed a prelude to finding perfect Love? Why were these people wasting their time with the ordinary, with the uneventful? Why were they not searching after their own perfect loves? Or, if they had already found love, then why were they here in this noisy place when they could be in some quiet peaceful setting enjoying that love?

What were they doing now? Oh, yes, the class yell:

We smoke dope! We slug rum!
We're the Class of Seventy-one!

Unbelievable, thought Timothy. It was just unbelievable—and sad. Why did these people glorify and put faith in fleeting escapes and temporary sanctuaries? Didn't they know that Love was out there? That It was the most wonderful escape, the purest sanctuary of all?

He thought about this for awhile, then returned his thoughts to his own reason for being here. And so, bending a little further forward on the bench, and still pretending to study the program, he peeked through his fingers and waited. He expected to be enraptured at any moment. He expected to behold his Special One emerging from out of the crowd and walking toward him with a radiant smile.

He watched and waited for Her appearance for several minutes; then, his eyes hurting from maintaining their upward position, he decided to relax his vigil for a while. He lowered his eyes to again look at the program. Deciding that he would prefer darkness over the bright paper and boring print, he shut his eyes and began to fashion scenes of embracing Toni amid surroundings more appealing to him.

Timothy was soon flying. Flying without wings, flying without effort. Up, up, up. Up past the planets, up past the stars. Up to a cool and quiet fairyland forest of great, swaying magical trees, where dwelt the Special One; She whose white robed figure he fell prostrate before, and whose ankles he clasped in adoration.

But then he was brought back to the bright, hot, and noisy gymnasium by a light sensation at his shoulder. Someone was touching him. Instantly straightening up, and dropping his hands from his brow, he, with face, for the first time, fully revealed, turned toward the direction of the touch.

It was the form of a young woman that filled Timothy's vision. She was very lovely, and she was smiling at him. Timothy blinked twice, and then, with his mouth slightly open, he was overwhelmed by the realization of whose presence he was now within. How many hours had he spent during the last ten years losing himself in these same eyes that now looked into his own? How many hours had he spent in study and admiration of the contour of this nose? The shape of these same lips? How many times had he kissed the image of this same face; this beautiful face that, as far as he could see—or as for as he allowed himself to see—ten years had done absolutely nothing to? The smiling presence above him was that of the Special One. She had come to him. He had finally found *Love, Itself*!

And now he saw those lips moving. He heard a sweet voice.

"I've been looking for you."

I've been looking for you.... Were those the words that that voice had uttered? Had that voice really spoken those wonderful words?

I've been looking for you! Yes! Of course those were the words—because Love *had* been looking for him! Had he not known this all along? *This,* then, was the rendezvous! *This* was the moment!

But what does one do when Love touches you and tells you that It has been looking for you? Timothy, who was now all emotion with only a vague awareness of his own identity, at first found himself powerless to do anything. For in that moment, time, space and everything else save that beautiful, smiling face did not exist for him. The radiant visage above him was his universe, and he seemed to be a tiny, tiny something existing solely for the sake of awe.

And it was at some point that he heard himself screaming out—

"Oh, Love, I've been looking for You, too, Love!"

It seemed to Timothy that the echo of his voice lingered and lingered within the gymnasium. He realized that he must have shouted *very* loudly—perhaps as loudly as he could. Because from the people gathered here, of whose presence he had again become aware, he heard not a single sound. And although he did not look around, he knew that every single pair of eyes there was staring at him.

But Timothy was neither ashamed nor afraid. For if Love stands with you, then who can stand against you?

But the lips! Now they were moving again. Listen! He must listen to the voice of Love!

"Uh...I—uh... I brought a name tag for you. I saw you come in, but you went by the table at the door so fast, I couldn't stop you. You see, everybody's supposed to wear a name tag, so when I had a chance, I had to find you and give you one. Also, there's an admission of twenty dollars. Uh...who are you? I mean, what's your name?"

What is one who wants to believe in, who *needs* to believe in, a special something to do when that something in which he has placed all his belief and hope and faith has failed him? What is one who trusted in the existence of something supernatural and sweet to do when there suddenly seems nothing beyond hard, indifferent logic—when there suddenly seems to be nothing beautiful and magical to care for you, to love you?

On a dark and lonely road there was an old Fairlane being driven by a young man named Timothy, who was all shattered and shriveled inside. He felt betrayed. He felt like a fool. He felt a great, gaping nothingness within his being. His mind was a vortex of wrenching thoughts spinning around and around and tormenting his sense of awareness. But he knew where he was, and although the recent past hardly seemed to have happened, he knew where he had been.

Yes, it all seemed like a bad dream, but he knew that it had happened because he hurt so badly within. He remembered the crowd, the noise, the heat, the lights. He remembered a certain girl that he thought he loved. He remembered a touch at his shoulder. He remembered shouting out with unleashed joy and with all his might a response to something this girl had said. He remembered the confused, uneasy expression on her face. He remembered her suddenly laying two articles, a pen and a blank name tag, beside him on the bench, and then, without a further word, nervously walking away. Then all was bleary. There was a vague memory of frantic flight from the scene. A blurred memory of swimming through a hot lake of humanity…of running at top speed down a pathway…of the screeching of tires…of white line segments streaking under in the middle of the highway. And he was at the present again.

But the present was icy, heavy, unendurable. Of what value was the present if there was nothing magical and sweet to care for you? Of what value was life, itself, if there was no Love to love you?

"No!" cried Timothy. And his vision at last began to blur. His stomach tightened, pushing up quivering, half vocal breaths, and wet pain flowed freely from his eyes. His attention returned to the white segments bisecting the highway and shooting by the car on the left. White streaks of paint on asphalt. Hard, cold, depressing—just like everything else. No Love at all.

"Oh, how can I go on, if You're not out there?"

And then, on a wild, desperate impulse, he pressed the accelerator as hard as he could. He would end it. He would get everything possible from this old car and then crash into something headlong.

There! Up ahead to the right! Something to give him release. It was a tree.

But this tree...why did it suddenly interest him? Why, in these last, slow motioned seconds did he wonder, or even care, what kind of tree this was? And a curious thing: Why did it suddenly seem...attractive? And then he suddenly knew what kind it was. It was a mimosa.

And what was this? Something returning to him. Something that he had completely forgotten about. A tingling, sweet sort of feathery feeling deep inside. This feeling! Could it, perhaps, suggest that he was desired?

What was this! The mimosa. It had vanished. Vanished! Faded from view. What was happening?

Wait! There! There it was again, just up ahead.

But how could all of this be happening? How in this mundane, concrete world could this be? Trees just didn't dissolve from one place and rematerialize in another. Could it be that he was home in bed having the most vivid dream in his life? Could it be that he was hallucinating? Or could it be, perhaps, that this world wasn't *quite* so mundane and concrete after all?

But why wonder about this? Why not wait and see what would happen? And in the meanwhile, look! Look how beautiful this tree was. And smell how pretty was its fragrance. Yes, the smell was in the car. It was every bit as sweet as that sensation, that growing sensation, somewhere in his heart. He must draw closer to this tree. He must satisfy an overwhelming longing to touch this tree. To embrace this mimosa—this mimosa that he now knew was somehow his own mimosa at home.

But it was gone again! Vanished once more!

But not for long; for now he could see it again. And this time he knew it was *not* an illusion. For he saw it by his house. It would not disappear again. And now that he knew that it would not vanish anymore—that it was now embraceable—it was more beautiful than ever.

Yes, how beautiful was this tree of life! How wonderfully did it sway in the wind; how charmingly did it play with the argentine moonlight. Why, it actually seemed to sparkle with silver. To twinkle like a Christmas tree. And the fragrance, growing ever stronger, was purely captivating. It was as if it wafted down from paradise itself. His whole being rejoiced in its deliciousness. And it seemed to be welcomed by the feathery sweetness within him as a source of strength.

This mimosa! What manner of special Something could it be? It was swaying…and sparkling…and beckoning…

It was just a little later, or, perhaps, just a little sooner, that he became oblivious to everything save the vision, rustling and fragrance of the silvery, moonlit mimosa. He did not remember slowing down, turning in and leaving the car. Indeed, anything about the past was now very difficult to remember. And nothing—nothing other than this tree seemed any longer important. Even his own identity, the remembrance of which had become very dim and distant, now seemed to matter very little. Nothing at all mattered anymore except this tree of eternity.

And then he was standing under the mimosa, looking up through the limbs towards the full, glorious moon overhead and rejoicing in the delicate, pleasing patterns formed by the branches. And he positively exulted in the aroma. The aroma! This rich, transporting flavor of mimosa blossom and much more. He knew that this was how the trees in paradise smelled. He breathed in deeply again and again, and felt his whole being enriched and enraptured by the sweet fragrance from without and by the sweet feeling from within.

But where, now, was the difference? Did fragrance and feeling not now seem one and the same?

Again and again and ever deeper he breathed it in; it was irresistible. And as he continued inhaling it he could sense how much something maybe wondrously pure and benign desired to have him…forever. And from this notion there billowed and fluffed up all within him an even more luscious ecstasy than before.

And now the wind stirred again. A cool little breeze gently swayed the shimmering tree and softly swished and whispered within the leaves. The mimosa was shimmering...and swaying...and whispering...whispering his name.

And he fell and embraced his mimosa. He hugged it tightly, tightly. And as he did so, it occurred to him how terrible it was to hate anyone—but how worse it was to hurt anyone. He discovered that he loved everyone in the world. There followed an understanding of how things that previously seemed important—money, competitiveness, politics, religion seemed superfluous, even ridiculous. And then the notion arose that even thought itself seemed unnecessary. Why, it even seemed to be drudgery! It seemed silly, and antiquated. And so he thought no more. He found it an easy thing to do. Yet, he remained aware even so. He was an awareness of both nothing and everything clasping the ankle of the most wondrous Something of all. He was an awareness clasping an ankle, and existing solely for the sake of AWE.

This awareness—which seemed somehow to be attuned to both nothing and everything—felt like a sparkling droplet of perfect sensation, felt itself being snatched out of something that seemed quite clumsy and easily perishable, and being drawn up with a grand, pulsating Deliciousness. And here within this Deliciousness, it found infinite pleasure in the presence of countless other awarenesses, which, like itself, were also sparkling droplets of perfect sensation. The whole Deliciousness Itself was Awareness, was Perfect Sensation. And just lately It had become just a tiny bit *more* aware and just a tiny bit *more* perfect.

The wind had died now. There was no longer even the least little breeze. But She of the Other Kingdom—it must have been LOVE—was swaying...and swaying...

Peace be with you.

CPSIA information can be obtained
at www.ICGtesting.com
Printed in the USA
LVHW112001050422
715401LV00006B/326

9 780578 384351